MEM

a novel

BETHANY C. MORROW

The Unnamed Press
Los Angeles, CA

The Unnamed Press
P.O. Box 411272
Los Angeles, CA 90041

Published in North America by The Unnamed Press.

1 3 5 7 9 10 8 6 4 2

Copyright © 2018 by Bethany C. Morrow

ISBN: 978-1-944700-55-3

Library of Congress Control Number: 2018931444

This book is distributed by Publishers Group West

Cover design & typeset by Jaya Nicely

To Beth, who knew immediately
that *Mem* was a keepsake

WEW

NO. 1

I am a memory. Now I suppose I'll live like one.

I received the telegram a week before I approached the receptionist's desk. A lovely girl was stationed there—a student, no doubt. What they call an undergraduate, which means she's naive. She might have mistaken me for a student as well, except that I handed her a wide, rectangular slip of paper that read: *Dolores Extract No. 1. You are hereby recalled to the Vault. Please return to the premises no later than noon, August 30, 1925.*

If she was shocked then, or intrigued, she made no mention of it. I found it strange, since in the eighteen years I've lived out in the city, among real people, they always have been. Anyone who finds out what I am cannot hide their fascination. I've learned also that when people are in awe, more often than not, they cannot resist telling you so directly. It becomes the way you distinguish one real person from another, by what stimuli force them to react.

Professor Toutant's gentle wife, Camille, was perhaps the first. Together with the Professor, she became something like an adoptive parent: a mother and a friend. Unlike the countless other real people I would meet, Camille's interest and the affection that soon followed were genuine. I knew by the way she spoke to me, as we exchanged stories about our lives and pasts and passions. While conversations with others quickly devolved into self-satisfying interrogations, Camille, from the beginning, gave something back. More than I could have expected, she sought out a relationship with me, campaigning for me to live outside the Vault and committing to funding my entire existence because my Source was disinclined. I was furnished with an apartment, and without hesitation she and the Professor set about filling it with things; things I never had occasion to use, or else—still being a young woman—I was oblivious when the opportunity arose.

I left nearly everything there, in my rented flat, when I received the recall. Whatever the reason the Vault wanted me back, I doubted I would ever need those things again. The kettle and the towels. The linens and the china, especially the china. In the underground complex sprawling beneath the university clinic, the Vault was a safe deposit for the clients who did not want their memories returning home with them. If nothing else—if there were no specific reasons for my recall—it simply meant I was returning to my proper role as a belonging again and I should need no more belongings of my own.

Still, from the twenty-third of August till the thirtieth, I rarely left my flat, trying on each frock, every hat and slipper, choosing only so many as would fit into the Gladstone bag gifted me by the Professor. Knowing that even one dress would be too many, I packed three just the same and, in the end, decided to smuggle a few things more. Memories of my very own. Professor and Camille would appreciate this—that I had brought them. They'd been witness to much of my city life; they would want to see which things I couldn't stand to leave behind when at last they came to visit.

Now, as I stood just past the receptionist's desk, my hands gripped the leather handles, darker by several shades than the stout bag attached to them. Safe inside my Gladstone, I felt each memento swell in significance given everything I'd left behind. I hesitated in the hallway, trying to decide whether to steal a glance inside the bag, to see what I had chosen, now that it was everything I owned.

A ticket stub from the movie theater down the line from my flat. I'd seen *The Toll of the Sea* every night for a week, and I'd saved every stub, afraid I'd forget, afraid that the dream that each night promised—the same dream I've had since the day I was extracted—would undo the day I'd lived before. I am a memory, but no expert on how they are born or by what ritual they are preserved. Still, I never tired of that movie, and it made me wonder if real people did. Perhaps my desire to watch it again and again gave me away. The ticket stub was a bookmark inside my favorite issue of *The Delineator*, a magazine to which I was introduced by Camille. She began a subscription for me as well. Eighteen years of beautiful covers and colors and words, but I always favored the first one she gave me.

Camille carried one issue or another with her everywhere, so that she'd have something to read when she visited her husband at the university, in his department office or else the one he kept in the clinic. I'd been extracted only two months before our meeting, after that horrible accident with the automobile, but even in that short time the staff and the students saw something unique in me. Something the other memories—or Mems, as they call us—did not have. It was why I was first allowed outside of the Vault for brief tours of the clinic or walks on the terrace, though always accompanied. On one such tour, the staff member drifted for more than a moment, and I took a seat next to Camille.

I remember tilting my head to admire the bright red gown worn by the woman on the cover of the magazine she was reading. The model was composing a letter, one gloved hand holding a postcard and the other lifting a pencil delicately to her chin. I found myself wondering what she was in the midst of writing, and to whom, before making a note of my own to relay that wondering to my Banker. He was always interested to hear such things.

"It's a lovely picture, I think." Camille's voice drew my gaze away from the magazine and then she lifted it as though to invite me back.

"Yes, it is. And the dress. I have one like that."

"Have you?" She smiled.

"Not precisely, but yes."

And then I caught sight of the plain frock I'd been issued. There was no corset, the entire dress seemingly made from one length of material, though the sleeves might have been an exception. The year was 1906 and even a memory knew that all of North America was watching the Northeast for the standard of city style.

"It was much nicer than what I'm wearing now," I said, without blushing. At the time, I wouldn't have known how, not organically. So recently extracted, no one would have begrudged a reliance on my Source's past and tendencies to sustain me in casual conversation. Instead, while I considered us equal proprietors over her memories, it seemed the present and the future should be entirely mine, and I took care to ensure that from now on my voice and mannerisms would be, too. As for Camille, a flicker of recognition crossed her face and she laid the magazine in her lap, a gloved forefinger keeping her place between the pages.

"I see. Then this is strange." She said the second phrase more quietly than the first. When she squinted, her plump cheeks overwhelmed her hazel eyes so that they seemed to vanish into the rosy pink of her face. "Where are you from?"

Like all Mems, the question prompted me to recount the memory that spawned me, and when she'd heard it, she said she thought her husband and I should meet.

Packed along with the ticket stub and my first issue of *The Delineator*—the model's long, slender pencil still lightly tapping her chin all these years later—was a robe. The robe was entirely special. Across the left breast was embroidered the name I'd given myself in thick-threaded cursive, red against ivory silk. To the rest of the world, I might always be Dolores Extract No. 1, named for my Source and the sequence in which I'd been extracted. But during the course of the week I'd spent in the darkened movie theater, watching *The Toll of the Sea*, I had become Elsie. Not because I so adored the film's character and certainly not because I resembled her in any way, but because there was so much about her left to know. And perhaps because, even with so much unsaid, her entitlement was assumed. Her place was never questioned.

The robe had been a present to myself, a reminder of who I really was. It had been a secret, even from Camille, but now it would tell everyone, Bankers and visitors alike, that recall or not I was not just any Mem.

"Do you need a guide?" the receptionist asked when she realized I was still there.

My hands twisted around the leather handles, massaging the oils from my palms into the already aged material.

"Not at all." My mouth closed, and I drew in a breath of air to steady myself. "I know the way."

It was down the far stairwell, where my heels clicked against the metal steps, lonely echoes failing to fill the space. My mind refused to relinquish my flat, the echo beginning to resemble the porcelain landscape of my en suite washroom. Every night, the violent sounds of my nightly dream had been washed away one teardrop at a time by the leaking faucet and the water pooling in the basin.

Click, click, click. Until despite the lack of windows, I knew I was underground. When I reached the bottom there was just one door, and I held the knob only to find myself drawn back to my own apartment's door and the hall outside of it. I should have forgotten to return the keys so that now I could hustle back and laugh with the nosy super over my absentmindedness. She would tease me for the time I'd been so excited to catch the trolley to a matinee that I'd left the door wide open. She would ask a thousand questions and, out of politeness, I'd be obliged to answer them all.

But I had not forgotten. The keys had been returned, the woman so uncharacteristically reserved that I wondered whether she knew what it meant to be recalled—that I was not a simple, starstruck girl after all. I withdrew my hand from the knob, parting my lips so that my breath could escape gently, and finally pressed one hand against either side of my head, as if the bell-shaped hat could fit any more snugly. The reprieve was over. On the other side was the Vault, or rather the great circular gate that secured it. I hadn't thought so before, but now it looked like an immovable stone securing a tomb. Of course, the last time I saw it, I was looking over my shoulder as it closed behind me. I had no reason to think it imposing then.

In the Vault, Banker is a title given to scientists. My first was an older gentleman with kind eyes and coal-black hair that parted down the center and seemed to swim away in glossy waves. There were lines around his mouth, I thought because he talked so much. Whenever he was in my dormitory, he spoke softly—to a gathering of students, to another Banker. Never to me, not at first. Not until we ventured aboveground together at the behest of the family. Once outside the Vault he seemed more able to see me. Underground, he always had the glint in his pale eyes—kind and expressive even when he was quiet, never cold—and the stern pressure above his eyebrows. There was also the slight turn of his head; then I knew he was uncomfortable with my looking at him. Uncomfortable with the fact that I could see him at all. That I, unlike his other wards, was aware of his presence. By the time more Dolores extracts had accumulated in the Vault, it had become clear that not only was I an anomaly, but also that my Banker was unsure how to respond to that fact.

From the outside, there was no question that I belonged belowground with the rest of them. The other Dolores Mems and I shared the same face and body, virtually an identical appearance altogether. Our Source aged well back then, and the three of us who were there before I left—myself, along with Dolores Nos. 2 and 3—were nearly the same age. Nineteen, nineteen, and twenty, there was nothing to distinguish us but an almost imperceptible difference in my skin and the chevron-shaped scar on No. 3's right index finger where she'd cut herself on the can opener. *She* hadn't done anything, of course; the real Dolores had, before extracting her.

I loved that can opener with the thick yellow handle and grip. It reminded me of our mother teaching us to cook. She'd taught us to be quite careful with it, and I wondered if Dolores's scar was at all related to why a third Mem existed, though I made certain never to ask. A part of me worried what I might hear about our mother and father if I ever questioned the origin of the third Mem. I worried I might learn that something horrible had happened to them, or to a dear friend, or to my kitten, Petunia, and I wanted to remember them all exactly as I did—though my Banker fixated on how I could. How *did* I recall so much? How did I recall anything besides the reason for my extraction? he would ask sometimes. Never mind that I shouldn't have been capable of replying; he seemed truly desperate to hear my answer, though it was never satisfactory. I could no more explain the existence of my memories and affections than my Banker could have explained his, but of course he would never be required to.

When I first entered the Dolores room, I had no time to acknowledge the three beds that remained in the same place as when I had left or the new source of light and color that seemed to emanate from somewhere overhead. My attention immediately fell to the one other Dolores in our dormitory. She lay on her bed with her whole body drawn into a ball and looked like she'd been recently crying. Or rather, she was depicting a time when our Source had been crying, since the tears didn't really belong to her.

After being away from the Vault for the better part of two decades, I had no idea how many Dolores extractions had come and gone, or why. Of course, I was still nineteen, as I always will be, but I knew that the real Dolores must be nearly thirty-nine now. To be quite honest, it hadn't occurred to me until my recall, until another Dolores was there in front of me. In all my years thinking about my Source, in the innumerable nights I'd dreamed of our last moments as one mind or of our solitary moment standing side by side, I never altered her. A real person might have envisioned herself progressing through age, imagining the changes her style and wardrobe and even her physique would undergo. But frozen in my own age, I kept her there with me. Just as a film preserved a romance while in real life the actors moved on, in my mind, Dolores was ever young because I was. I never considered how she would look at twenty-one or twenty-five or her late thirties. And while I presumed that the Dolores on the bed was a recent extraction, I couldn't say if she'd been lying there a year or a day. After all, I wasn't entirely sure what thirty-eight looked like, not to the point of accurately assigning it to anyone. The huddled extract may have been thirty-eight or thirty-one, if she wasn't younger still. What I did know for sure was that she would not last much longer.

The Mem's skin was dim. Especially where her elbows bent, curving around the legs drawn to her breast, it had already faded from my deep brown to a hollow gray and then cracked. Her eyes were pools of black into which her lashes and eyebrows seemed to be sinking, and the blackness seemed almost to bleed into her once dark skin. Her hair should have been a bright copper, like our mother's. Instead it was a sour shade of yellow, and while I and the Dolores I'd known wore our hair shiny and pressed, this fading extract had a short bob of wispy frizz. I rather liked the hairstyle itself, preferring it to the long, tiresome styles of my own, bygone year when a woman's hair was her crowning glory and achievement. What I could not imagine was that my Source would want to be seen with her stylishly short hair in such a state, even if only by Bankers and staff. I couldn't imagine that her father would be pleased either.

I didn't speak to the Mem, only proceeded to the farthest bed and deposited my bag. After that I couldn't decide what to do. If she were anyone else, at least if she were a real person, I could have tried to console her. Even if she'd been a stranger, I would have drawn a handkerchief from the purse I usually carried and offered it without question. I'd insist that she keep it, petting her arm and cooing any number of comforting phrases, whether she kept her burdens to herself or fell into my consoling arms.

But she was a Mem. She would not answer me, or else when she did her words would be noticeably out of context. She was trapped in a single moment, whichever had been too unpleasant for the real Dolores to bear. She and every other memory were, quite literally, single-minded, replaying themselves every minute of every hour of the day and then watching their origins at night.

A coldness pricked me in my midsection then and I tried to ignore it. If I succumbed—if I listened to the small voice inside my head reminding me that the latter of those conditions applied to me as well—I may have slipped headlong into an anxiety from which I feared I could not escape, now that I was back. So I tried also not to notice that the armoire into which I began hanging my clothes had been empty. There was no need for running a warm cloth around the interior, as Camille had done when moving me into my own place in the city. Running my hand along the bottom before setting my bag inside, I felt no mothballs, no wayward string or button. This Dolores would leave nothing, as the ones before had not. It would be as though no one had been here. Only Mems. Only us.

From the doorway, I looked up and down the hall, relieved that I couldn't see the Vault gate from our dormitory. At either end was another hallway, and for a long time, no one passed to my left or right, not even in the distance. There was little sound, unless I closed my eyes and strained to hear something, and even then the clearest sign of life was Dolores's abbreviated breathing.

Back at my bed, I first sat leaning against the headboard, facing the open door, until I realized how alike we looked, my knees bent, my legs drawn into my chest, and my arms wrapped around them. The coldness pricked me again and I felt my resolve weaken. *This* was reality. I was not an honorary Banker, as the joke had gone, or the Professor's beloved assistant. I was, and had always been, their subject. The Vault was where their subjects lived and expired.

It was pitiful the way I had to cover my mouth to keep from sobbing. The tears I couldn't control; I could only turn away so that the other Dolores didn't see. I lay down on top of the blankets and pulled them around me. It was just after noon, but I closed my eyes and welcomed the replay of my horrible spawning memory. At least *that* was only a dream.

I awoke to stillness. It must have been night. The door was closed, the overhead lights put out. There were no windows through which I could see the natural moon, but above each of the three beds, there were colored glass windows behind which lights shone as though to take the moon's place. They had not been there in 1906 when I was extracted or in the fall of 1907 when I was discharged; neither could they bring a Mem much comfort unless the extract knew the sun and moon existed—and they weren't aware that anything did.

Something had changed while I slept—I knew without having to be told—but I stayed in bed for a moment, pretending it hadn't. Avoiding a glance at the now silent Dolores in the other bed, I lay in mine, wrapped in my blanket like a child who'd swaddled herself. I admired the light made lavender and pink and green by the glass, and had no way to know whether the hour was too unreasonable to find a student or a Banker. But then, I wasn't certain I had a use for reason anymore. The other Dolores certainly didn't.

I found someone at a station two halls over, her crisp white cap pinned notably farther back on her head than it should have been. Something about the woman, the ill-fitting nature of her uniform, made me guess she was new.

Or maybe it was simply the music playing too loudly on the radio on her desk.

"Congratulations," I ventured.

She seemed nervous even before her eyes met mine. "I beg your pardon?"

To my disappointment, she turned a knob on her radio and the festive music that poured from the lovely cone speaker and felt so out of place in this hall reduced to a whisper.

"I thought you must be new." When she didn't answer, I continued, wanting to put her at ease. "There were no nurses here when I left. None that I noticed, at least. I was never sure why they entrusted such work to students, but it seems they've finally gotten wise, wouldn't you say? In any case, just now I was looking for a Banker."

"None are available at this hour. I'm sorry," she said, one hand flitting about the fringe on her forehead while the other turned the knob again, reducing the volume even more. It must have been nervousness at the chatty Mem hovering at her station that kept her from switching it off completely, as the end of the day's programming had just been announced and the radio now fizzed with white noise.

"It must be midnight then," I said with a smile that I kept tethered to my lips in an effort to engage her.

The expression seemed to have the opposite effect.

"I listen to CKAC at home," I continued. "I've heard rumors of a new piano program this fall and I hope I won't have to miss it."

I stopped myself when her eyes drifted away from me, her discomfort palpable.

"Is something the matter?" she finally asked.

"Oh, no. It's just that a Dolores has expired." The friendly smile I'd had plastered to my face now felt strangely inappropriate, and I quickly removed it. "And I don't think I can sleep while she's there."

The receiver was nearly shaken from its cradle before she had the phone steadily in hand. Squeezing the black candlestick, she thrust her mouth to the rim of the transmitter, her voice breaking as she spoke to the operator.

Before her call was complete, the nurse asked that I wait outside my dormitory with the promise that someone was on their way, but it was only so I'd leave her be. I couldn't blame her for disliking me; feeling out of sorts in front of a Mem must have been infuriating, especially for someone who likely knew who I was, but hadn't been quite prepared to interact with me. When she, the Banker, and another man appeared in the hall, wordlessly passing me to enter my own room, the nurse blithely monitored her clipboard rather than acknowledge me.

"How long ago did she expire?" the Banker asked in a soft voice.

"I called you as soon as I was told," the nurse answered in an equally soft voice.

"By whom?"

Hushed whispers then, as though the nurse could sense the way I pressed myself to the wall at the edge of the doorframe, straining to hear them. To hear him.

"Miss?"

My face went hot and I drew myself back from eavesdropping, lest he approach the doorway and find me out.

"Miss?" he called once more, and I stepped into the opening. "Would you come in, please."

The nurse swept her hand across her fringe, almost as though saluting.

"Where are you from?" the Banker asked.

My cheeks still felt hot, and I could neither meet his pale eyes nor escape the expectancy in hers.

"The eleventh of August, 1906," I said at last. "I saw a man killed on the street by an automobile." Pulling back my shoulders and glancing once at the nurse, I continued: "I'm Extract No. 1."

"Of course," the Banker replied. "I only had to ask for the record."

"Of course," I echoed. If there was a record—and my testimony on it—I should be thorough. "I returned earlier today. Or yesterday, I should say." At that, he made an acknowledging sound.

"Were you awake when she expired?"

"I don't know exactly when it occurred. But she was nearly gone when I arrived."

The nurse's gaze leaped on me, and I stopped short of describing the symptoms of expiration that she should certainly have noticed. If she'd been intimidated by me at the nurses' station, she now seemed to have settled on disdain. For his part, the Banker exhaled audibly.

"She expired quite quickly for a memory like hers," he said, speaking as if to himself. "I feel certain the duration has something to do with the condition of the Source."

I caught at his statement but didn't speak while he tapped his chin with a ballpoint pen.

"But then, she was a reprint. Maybe that's all it takes."

While the third silent member of their team lifted the shell in his arms, the nurse placed a long white bag on the bed, and the expired Mem was placed inside and the bag fastened shut. I'd remained because I hadn't been excused, though I'd been careful not to appear interested. It was a behavior I'd learned in my years outside the Vault, blending into the background so as to avoid notice. A strategy, I've come to believe, that serves real people as well as it serves Mems.

When the silent man transported the Dolores from the room, the Banker spoke again and stopped the nurse as she was preparing to go.

"Has Dolores No. 1 been examined since returning, at least?"

She made a sound, the way one does to put off responding, her fingers strumming through the sheets in her file. "A day nurse would have made the exam."

"But would the record be there?" My voice didn't break, though my gaze did when she glanced up at me. "Or do we all share a single file?"

The Banker took a seat on the bed between my own and the one belonging to the recently expired Mem, tapping his chin again. The gesture reminded me of that first cover of

The Delineator, of Camille, and of my life outside, all at once. And the memory of that life—that, despite how far away it felt already, it had in fact existed—reminded me that I was underground now. The walls were tightening around me by the moment and I was in the Vault, for any number of bureaucratic reasons, but only one that mattered: because I was not real.

The Banker, coming out of his thoughts, turned to look at me with an unreadable expression. He couldn't know how the cold in my stomach had turned to revulsion. Mems didn't warrant funerals, which must have been why no one thought it morbid to search me for signs of expiration immediately after taking another Mem's shell away.

"They do share a file," he said, when I felt he might not speak again. "Every Dolores. Except you. Nineteen years later and you are still the only one."

The room was still then, the nurse paused with her fingers between the pages.

"I'll only be a moment." The nurse left us to search whatever cabinet housed the singularly unique file of Dolores's first extract. Never mind that if asked, I might have told her there was no record to find. I hadn't been visited since my arrival, by a day nurse or anyone else. And, present circumstances notwithstanding, I could not imagine anyone had thought it permissible to examine me in my sleep. Whether that assumption was reasonable, I couldn't know.

I didn't expect him to stay. When the Banker didn't leave, instead breathing deep and stretching his neck and shoulders, I moved to sit on the edge of the expired Mem's bed to face him.

"You have your father's eyes," I told him.

They brightened just slightly meeting my own. "I have his last name as well. But being who you are, you probably noticed the resemblance first."

The tag that hung over the right breast of his jacket listed his post and his name. Harvey Parrish.

"My father spoke of you quite a lot."

Now I looked at the linoleum floor to interrupt the swelling inside me. I felt so full at the thought that I worried I might spill over in front of him. Full at the thought that if he could not always talk to me, the elder Parrish had at least talked about me. Full at the sudden desire to tell my former Banker everything that I'd seen and done since the last time I saw him, since he'd suggested I might do well someplace beyond the Vault. Full of something more somber, too: that of the thousands of things I had owned in my life outside, I now had just three mementos of that time.

"He's..." I began but couldn't finish.

"Expired," Harvey said.

"Memories expire," I said, two tears slipping down my face and beneath my chin. "I know the difference between Mems and real people."

"Of course." He took a handkerchief from his pocket as he crossed between the beds and sat beside me. And Harvey Parrish offered it to me.

"I was very fond of him, that's all." I dabbed at my eyes, freeing drops that clung to my lashes before folding the handkerchief and offering it back. He would not accept it, and a moment later our silence was interrupted by the nurse's return. Clipboard still in hand, I thought she was startled by the scene and I hid his handkerchief in my fist.

"I'll let you get on with it." Harvey stood and I slowly followed suit. "But I'll be back in the morning. In the proper morning." He smiled at me, cupping the side of my arm and then quickly retracting his touch as though I'd stung him. The smile tapered and his gaze flitted around the room, then he was walking rigidly to the doorway.

"Harvey," I said before he passed through it, the nurse staring wide-eyed at him. "Banker Parrish. What's a re-print?"

His face was solemn when he turned back. "I'm used to speaking freely in the Vault. It was inconsiderate; I'm sorry."

For a brief moment I thought he meant to have a seat again and answer the question I'd asked and others I hadn't. Instead he addressed the nurse.

"I'll return in the morning."

And while she approached and he retreated, I could not imagine showing Harvey Parrish my memories or expect that he might appreciate the name I'd given myself. Besides his eyes and jet-black hair, he shared his father's discomfort, no matter how well they spoke of me. As the nurse began her examination, the handkerchief Harvey'd given me dampened in my tight grasp.

NO. 2

For one evening in 1922, I was the toast of Montreal. At least Camille said so. The Mount Royal Hotel was debuting, and the Professor and his wife swept me into the starlit night with promises that the glamourous event would rival any I'd seen on the silver screen. In fact, they'd no doubt that the affair would be so significant as to find itself *up there*, and that I might soon be both in the theater as a patron and on the newsreel as a star. The thought was intoxicating.

Even for the sophisticated city, the hotel was an over-whelming sight, imposing against the night sky in a bold presentation that began with a street-long treatment of awnings and arched windows. It seemed as wide as it was high, the broad face broken into three. On the street below the breathtaking architecture, horseshoes clipped along, mingling with the automobiles that deposited their cargo beneath the blinding lights or else carried envious passersby on their way.

But I was there, taking the Professor's hand and closing my borrowed stole around me with the other as I stepped out of the car. That was borrowed as well, the Professor said. A sleek black 1921 center door sedan that the Gray-Dort automobile company hoped he'd be tempted into purchasing. Regardless, lending it to us for an event as distinguished as the Mount Royal Hotel's debut would no doubt be a kind of advertisement for them, reinforcing Gray-Dort over Ford as "Canada's Choice." I felt at the height of celebrity, and even when my feet found the curb I wasn't certain I was on the ground.

"There are a lot of people anxious to meet you, Dolores," the Professor said as we stepped inside.

"She's here to enjoy herself, dear."

"And she will, darling. I promise." The Professor gently nudged me on when the glittering chandelier just inside the entrance bewitched me, stopping me in my tracks. Its light splashed across the ceiling and cascaded into the room beyond. "There's more, ma petite," he said with a smile, "there's more."

The "more" he described seemed to be people; they swam about the hotel in graceful parties, gloved fingertips touching jacket arms, bare necks bowing like swans'. They were all important, I could tell by their almost competitively straight posture and by the way their gentle laughter and delicate perfume lingered in the air. If they were expecting me, it was as the Professor's pride and joy, the jewel in his already acclaimed practice.

Memory extraction had brought the Professor international commendation in his discipline, but his case study of the extract who defied convention brought him social notoriety. In the intervening years since that night, Sources would occasionally appear at functions I attended with the Professor, parading their perfectly ordinary Mems around at parties, hoping to replicate that notoriety and the bygone celebrity afforded the original Dolores Extract No. 1.

Inevitably the Professor would be forced to engage the imposing Source and her Mem, who could be visiting from elsewhere in the Americas, or Madagascar, or anywhere really, since the wealthy were traveling from all over the world for extractions, and who always wondered aloud whether this or that delightful Mem might be the new face of his department. The Professor's answer was always the same: he was pleased that the technology was bringing relief and sometimes even amusement to the affluent classes, but he regretted the way his work remained financially inaccessible to others. The science of extraction had been developed to help people heal from painful memories, he reminded them, and the poor had as many as the wealthy. The cost of the Vault and Mem maintenance were understandably prohibitive, there was no escaping that, but in fact, his research showed that these happy pairs—the Sources who voluntarily visited his office with their Mems hoping to become the focus of some study or another—did not reflect the whole. The overwhelming majority of extractions continued to be exercises in purging, and few Sources retained their extracted memories as keepsakes. In truth, few Mems were of the happy sort, and their shelf life was expected to be relatively brief (or so the Bankers' observations had seemed to prove). Despite what others might say, he always concluded with a smile, there was but one Mem as old as the department itself. One whose resilience made a mockery of the notion that a Mem expired more quickly when the spawning memory was a troubling one. Just one Mem who knew she was a Mem, who knew something outside the memory because of which she'd been extracted.

That night in 1922, scientists and journalists, philanthropists and curious socialites, would watch me the way I'd so often watched them.

"I've been following your work quite closely," said a dowager, a decadent fan of ostrich feathers sweeping the air between her and the Professor. Over her shimmering, straight gown, she wore a splendid mink coat that put all others to shame. Between her wealth and refinement, the woman appeared to have aged with remarkable grace. She wore her pale face powder with understated mascaro and light rouge, but she forewent the more youthful pretense of lip-shaping. To her credit, she kept them a more distinguished, muted shade and made no attempt to a perfect cupid's bow.

The Professor politely dipped his head in her direction when she spoke, as every word of an even moderately cordial conversation was shared under the guise of great discretion by women of her class.

"I have something of a creative inheritance in mind for my children, you see, and after seeing Dolores for myself, my mind is made up." Her eyes never left him, but her hand arched over my wrist. If it actually touched, it was so delicately that I couldn't tell. Stranger still, as Camille was neither scientist nor subject, the dowager didn't seem to acknowledge her presence at all. "And, of course, I know how important reliable funding is in the sciences. My late husband was quite insistent that it not go overlooked in times of peace and excitement."

She fascinated me, to say the least. The way she seemed harmless and almost silly, the way I knew she couldn't have been. It wasn't only the way she held the Professor and Camille's rapt attention, but the way others made unspoken salutation in passing or else congregated in her peripheral view so as to be the very next to gain an audience.

She was in no way self-conscious and easily drifted from the subject of her husband's political position to her recent consideration that the Professor's research may not have been precisely what her husband had in mind when he encouraged her to support scientific advancements. She only finally hinted at her desire when she'd engaged us for the better part of an hour. Her expression became serious. "As I'm sure you know, my father endured dementia in his autumn years, brought on one would think by a hardening of the arteries. It isn't a graceful topic of conversation, but you're a man of science, we can be honest. It changed him entirely, so much so that my mother could not entertain, but at first it was only the most minute alteration. Little things which, of course, I won't bother you with."

She stopped herself, hemming and lifting her chin as though to avoid some pungent odor. Where her voice had been, orchestra music swelled in from another room, and in a moment, she began to smile.

"And I have what I think is a most creative inheritance in mind for my children, which news of Dolores has inspired, and what with this business of someday rationing extractions, as though we're at war. Well! I do hope you'll make a moment for me in your office on Monday, before tea."

Of course, the Professor agreed immediately, as though he knew his entire schedule offhand and was certain there would be nothing to conflict with her request, and the dowager took her leave to enjoy the night's festivities.

The mysterious proposal intrigued me, and as I was introduced and admired and offered assorted hors d'oeuvres, my mind returned to the Professor's office and what might soon transpire there.

"Camille will never forgive me if you don't enjoy yourself," he whispered as we stood politely for a reporter and his photographer.

"But I am, very much. It's everything I've dreamed."

He gave me a knowing look. It was no use denying my distraction to him. "You take too much after me," he said, hugging me with one arm, to the photographer's delight. "But work will have to wait."

When I smiled and hugged him back, our spectators cooed and offered us delighted applause.

On Monday, the Professor learned that the dowager had three memories to extract. They were all to be taken at once, three fond recollections from her years of being courted by her late husband, before time could destroy them. Camille told me that when the Professor expressed hesitation at taking three memories in such a short period, the dowager confessed what the couple had suspected that night at the hotel.

"It appears my father's condition is becoming mine. Slowly, as yet, but. A fractured mind is not a concern, Professor, it appears to be an inevitability."

"Then, if I may, would you not prefer to keep your happiest memories for as long as possible?"

"Legacy, Professor, is something my family has always held dear. Publicly, of course, you may simply refer to me as a trendsetter, if that will settle curiosity." Camille said the Professor thought the dowager seemed prouder of that possibility than she cared to confess. "I will treasure these memories as long as I feel it's safe to and then employ you discreetly. I want the children to be surprised."

Of course the Professor said he'd do his very best to honor the dowager's wishes. Chief among them was that the memories should be kept at the Vault, despite her means to care for them herself, because she intended one of them to go to each of her two daughters and only son. It was also because she hoped that by keeping them, the Professor might guarantee they could share my longevity. She'd seen ordinary Mems, of course, and knew one or two Sources who enjoyed entertaining with them. And while she enjoyed a good memory presentation as much as anyone, she felt entirely convinced that *her* Mems could be different. They could be like me. Certainly the Professor impressed upon her the fact that he could make no such guarantee and that he was entirely unsure why Dolores Extract No. 1 showed no signs of expiration, but life had taught the woman that all things were possible, as long as you made clear your reasonable desire.

I met them, the dowager's Mems, on the second day of my recall to the Vault. They were referred to as the Keepsakes, and it seemed possible that the older woman had in fact made something extraordinary, though it wasn't clear to what extent.

The Keepsakes were strange, even to me, if only because they were always together. I saw them first when they swept merrily past my open door and I was drawn as much to their ethereal sighs as to the parasols they each carried. The sight of those pastel accessories paired with the dowdy dresses the Vault required us to wear was too curious to ignore, and I hurried to the hall for a second look.

The fact that they still existed was not yet impressive. They were fond memories and only three years old, on the short end of the life expectancy for happy Mems. Whether they were self-aware was what prompted the staff to observe them obsessively, for though they never spoke except to whimsically utter their lover's name, those utterances seemed to prompt or intensify their collective sighs.

The evening that the eldest Keepsake plucked a down feather from another's loose hair, Harvey and a congregation of students descended on the sitting room for further observation. It hardly looked like science. There were no test tubes or gloves, as in the newsreels. They wore no protective glasses. Mostly, Harvey instructed one student or another to sit increasingly closer to the three and then, when the girls made no response, all members of the staff scribbled furiously. After that, they tried standing in what appeared to be the trio's line of sight. Again, the girls made no reaction, and again, the men annotated their annotations.

Finally, I approached, sitting beside the eldest.

"Hello."

She didn't respond. I turned to Harvey, who'd said nothing of my intrusion.

"May I have a feather?"

He delegated the task of retrieval to a member of his team, and when a pillow was dissected and the feather given, I put it in my hair. The eldest took no notice. Removing it from my own, I went to the Keepsake seated next to her and placed the feather in her hair instead. I only had time to step back before the eldest smiled, lovingly pulling it out again. Behind me, there was a symphony of scribbling. When I turned, the gathered men looked at me expectantly.

"I think it's part of her memory," I concluded.

"Something he did for her."

"Or maybe she did it herself," a second staff member posited over the theory of the first. "Maybe while looking in the mirror."

"That's why she only sees it when it's in one of her look-alikes' hair."

"Get a mirror."

Harvey had yet to look away from me.

"Did that help?" I asked when he didn't offer thanks.

The deep breath he took drew his head slightly back. "Yes. Thank you, Dolores."

I waited in my dormitory for Harvey's daily visit. Despite what I knew of Vault protocol, his visits had not proved daily yet. He hadn't come that morning or afternoon, though I'd heard him in the hall a number of times. He'd never come the day before, when the proper morning had begun. What I knew of real people's behavior gave me hope that now, because of my intrusion in the sitting room, he would be obliged to. He was, after all, my Banker.

"I'm sorry for yesterday," he said.

It seemed one moment he'd not been there and the next he was. I wondered if somehow I'd managed to slip into a dream with my eyes wide open; otherwise how could I have watched the door so intently and yet been surprised to see him standing there.

"Why didn't you come? I thought because I made you uncomfortable."

At that he blushed, and on his skin, it was all the more apparent.

"Why should you make me uncomfortable," he both asked and stated, walking farther into the dormitory and running a hand over his hair. "No, I was held up elsewhere."

It was the first time I'd been lied to by a man, that I knew of, and I felt it must mean something. What surprised me most was that while he was the one being dishonest, I somehow was the one made to feel small and uncertain.

"How did I do?" I asked, after balling my fists against the threat of cowardice. When he only looked on quizzically, I was forced again to speak explicitly. "On my exam, the night I arrived. Am I expiring now?"

"No, Dolores." Though he used that name, it was softened by the concern in his voice and by the way he stepped in my direction. "Not that we can tell."

A shudder of relief sent my hand to my chest as though I could hold myself together.

"Did something make you think you were?"

"She didn't say," I said of the nurse. "She didn't speak a word to me after you left."

"She wouldn't be accustomed to talking to Mems or having them talk back."

"But you are?"

Instead of replying, Harvey's lips rested, his face unreadable again. While male actors on-screen tended to gesticulate and pantomime—sometimes wildly—by comparison the Banker was impressively reserved. I was never sure of his thoughts, even when he spoke.

"Professor rarely took my photo anymore, not with the examination equipment. He knows my skin by heart and my Source's too, so it's been some time since I've seen

Dolores and I compared. We were the same shade when I was extracted, did you know?"

Of course he knew. That fact had been the single outward clue that I was different from the others, albeit in hindsight. While every other Mem began life slightly paler than their Source, I hadn't. At the time, my original Banker and his team had decided that there were too many variables to say definitively if my pigmentation and consciousness were at all related, given that I was extracted so soon after the memory that spawned me. Now, when most Sources extracted memories from further in their past and differences in their coloring were attributable to any number of things, determining the significance of my complexion was harder still.

"I'd like to see them now," I told Harvey. "The examination pictures the nurse took. To know for myself what will become of me."

"Are you changing, Dolores?" His tone was academic. He may as well have had his writing pad in hand, prepared not to listen but to keep a detailed record.

"Perhaps. But if my skin is fading, it's because I'm underground."

"Away from sunlight?"

"No." I resisted the frustration threatening to silence me. If Harvey Parrish could change my fate, whatever it was, I had to plead my case. "Away from freedom. I never felt I might expire until now, that's all I know for sure."

"Your color hasn't changed," he said with the reserve I was beginning to consider uniquely his. "It's precisely the shade of brown it was the day you were extracted. The same is true of your hair and eyes. And it's nothing short of remarkable, Dolores. That's the truth."

I noticed when his eyes flicked away and, at my noticing, he cleared his throat.

"But if you'd like to see for yourself, I'll have the pictures shown to you."

I breathed, as calmly as I did whenever I wore my silk robe with Elsie's embroidered name. With his promise, the garment felt close, though it still hung in the closet. And despite that I knew so little of her, no matter that I'd seen *The Toll of the Sea* numerous times, I knew she was the one to be envied. Elsie was the real girl, born in the same world as the man who loved her and perhaps loved for no more reason than that. Especially now, when I was alone with Harvey for a second time, Elsie was the one I wanted to be.

"I met that dowager," I said suddenly. "A few years ago. It's remarkable to see her in the Keepsakes, looking so young. I only hope they'll be the legacy she intended, if ever her children decide they want them."

He nodded but didn't appear to be listening, no matter how informed I proved myself to be. Unlike the Professor or my Banker before him, my interest in the discipline did not inspire him to energetic conversation. Standing in my dormitory, waiting to see whether his attention would return, I was trapped not just by the Vault but by the constant reminders that it was far better to be a real person. If I were a real girl, I'd know whether this discomfort I felt meant I wanted him to go or to stay.

"How old are you?"

He drew in a breath to answer. "Twenty-five."

"Isn't that funny? That I'm nineteen but so much older than you."

"But you shouldn't be." Now he seemed to come out of his thoughts and face me, his curiosity evident in the tone of his voice. "You weren't extracted until ought-six. You shouldn't recall anything before then, not even what the real Dolores knows. You shouldn't retain anything that happened after."

"But I do."

For a moment there was nothing beyond us, me smiling through my discomfort. His pale eyes glimmered so that I thought there might be a smile inside them. And then he broke the spell.

"I'm going to tell you, now, why you were recalled. I've never had to before, but then there was never a Mem who worried over her own test results."

"You're making me nervous, Harvey."

"Don't say that," and as he turned it away, his face was stern again.

"Don't say what?"

"My name."

My heart played a game of leapfrog inside my chest, an almost audible pulse hopping at the back of my throat. Harvey looked at me, the pained expression gone, and whatever he'd been ready to say, I could tell he'd changed his mind.

"The staff will think it strange if you do."

In my life outside the Vault, I'd learned the many reasons real people laugh and in how many ways a laugh can result. Just this moment, I laughed because my fear over my test results was followed and outdone by Harvey's own cowardice. And while I'd been brave and candid with him, I knew he had not been. Whyever he didn't want me calling him by his given name, it wasn't on behalf of the staff.

"Does the staff not think me ridiculous as it is? But what would you prefer? Banker?" I made the word intentionally ridiculous. "What could be more sober?"

"No." It almost seemed he recognized the line I'd quoted. "No, I suppose the staff will grow accustomed to whatever you call me."

The pleasant irregularity in my pulse returned.

"I suppose they will." I smiled. "But what does my Source call you, anyway? Doctor? Perhaps I'll call you that."

He snorted.

"She doesn't call me anything anymore. It's been years since she recognized me at all."

The frog caught, stopping my heart between beats. If I were my victrola with the flower-stenciled horn, it was like the music had ended and all that remained was the sound of the needle skating along inside the groove.

"She's fractured?"

He pressed his lips together.

"Harvey."

I closed my eyes, unable to stop the pain that followed—not the very real tightening in my chest or the phantom cold I'd felt upon finding an expiring Dolores. I could only breathe through it and know that it was overwhelming just this moment, but that this moment would pass. I opened my eyes and found Harvey staring at me with a wrinkled brow.

"How many extractions has she had?"

"At least two dozen since you."

"What about the restriction the dowager spoke of?"

"It was only a ballot then. It passed, of course, but still. It has taken some time to enforce."

"But it meant she could only extract three memories in a five-year period."

"No. Even if it had been imposed, it meant she could only create three Mems."

It seemed at first as though Harvey had repeated my words back to me, but I knew his small distinction mattered by the way his eyes steadied. He was preparing to explain and I couldn't look away, though I didn't have the luxury of discarding what memories I couldn't manage. Whatever he said—of my Source, of what she'd done—I would have to keep.

"The problem is the language of the law," he said, while I focused on the hand he swept through his hair. "Isn't it always. The restriction was shortsighted. It focused on safeguarding people from the damage we believed was most a threat when extracting the Mem container, which is something like the memory, and the afterbirth, and maybe even a piece of the mechanism that conceives. It's matter that makes the Mem robust but leaves the Source stripped, at least when overdone. But Sources are well within their rights to reprint new memories over existing Mems, provided they have one that hasn't begun to expire, and that procedure is far less taxing. Dolores is no exception. Perhaps even if she's no longer of sound mind." He crossed his arms and then detangled them. "Two dozen doesn't begin to estimate the number of procedures she's actually had. I'm afraid in her case, overdone is perhaps an understatement."

The Professor hadn't told me such a thing existed. We talked often of the department and his work: the way they had begun stretching and changing society itself, and how we would have to come to terms with what these new creatures actually were—if they were or were not people; if they were possessions; if emotions could be put aside and appearances were in fact deceiving. I say "we" because he always allowed me to feel an integral part of it all, rather than one of "them." Because he promised I was outside of it now, in my robe and my movie theater, my galas and my apartment. But if he'd never mentioned that Sources could and probably had been reprinting Mems all this time, it could only mean he worried what the advancement would mean for me.

"There is a way to print a new memory over a Mem," I said, to anchor myself in the conversation at hand.

Harvey sat on the bed across from mine.

"How does it change them? Us?" And before he could answer, I shivered. "Does it hurt?"

The question was like a starter shot sending a runner out across the track. Harvey's hand was suddenly over mine, his pale eyes glistening like pools of water.

"Is that why I've been recalled? So that she can reprint me?"

"We can't afford to let that happen, Dolores."

"Don't say that," I said. "It isn't my name."

"Has someone given you another?"

"I have. My name is Elsie."

And when he lifted his hand to cup one side of my face, I was surprised.

"You are remarkable. Elsie."

NO.3

The next time Harvey Parrish came to my dormitory, he brought two photographs of me: one the nurse had taken the week before, the night the Dolores extract expired; the other his father had taken. The recent photo was cast aside for the one I hadn't expected him to bring. Immediately I felt its weight and significance; it returned to me so easily that I wondered what had kept it away till now.

"I'd just woken up," I told him, eyes anchored on the earliest evidence that I was unlike every previous Mem. In the photograph, I was still lying on the cold steel stretcher so unlike the well-padded one Dolores inhabited. She was out of focus—I being the reason the elder Parrish had paused in his examination to take the photo in the first place—but I could see that she was still asleep. Only my eyes were open. Only my head turned on the gurney to look at the lens as though into a pair of eyes. "Your father was the first thing I saw, once I was outside Dolores. He heard my first words."

"I'm cold."

I looked at Harvey, sitting on the bed across from mine, leaning toward me in a way he hadn't before. "How did you know?"

He turned the photo in my hand, and there on the back, in lovely script that must've been his father's, were my first words in quotes. There were other words as well. Notes he'd written about me. A mention of my skin, of the way I was no paler than my Source—and beneath that, something more.

She is something new.

She. And elsewhere, *her*. Never *it*.

I wiped the tear from my cheek and closed my eyes for a moment to recall the way my first Banker's awe had slowly blossomed into a smile. Then he'd offered me a blanket. Now, his son went to my pillow and retrieved the handkerchief he'd given me the week before. His handkerchief that now belonged to me. He said nothing about how I'd hidden it half beneath my pillow, folded into the beginnings of a linen airplane.

"Thank you," I said when he offered it to me, but I did not dab the inner corners of my eyes, only looked at the folded kerchief in my hands and remembered. "There was one other photograph," I told him. "One of both Dolores and me."

I didn't have to close my eyes to see the summer of 1907, though the Vault had neither its blessedly slight humidity nor the day's endless bright blue sky. I glanced at the low ceiling and saw through it to billowy clouds and a coolness sweeping off the Saint Lawrence River. There on its banks waiting for the air show to begin, I'd stood with the original Banker Parrish, and when Dolores approached, she was holding her father's hand but looking only at me. While he refused to acknowledge my presence, I was the reason Dolores had come. Had she been braver, perhaps she would have said so, or anything to me.

"My father loved aeronautics," I told Harvey without turning my attention to him. "Perhaps you know that. He said that it—like science—was not a common man's hobby. Once I was separated from Dolores I took the statement more seriously. I could see that his delight in things that set him apart explained his love of aviation, at least to some extent. I think he liked the fact that flight—like Mem extraction—is costly. That neither are sports that everyone can enjoy."

"You thought that once extracted. But not before?"

He was writing something down and it almost made me stop. I breathed in the fragrance of the water, a pleasant piece of the memory from that August day, and laid the handkerchief aside.

"I found him very different once I was on my own. When I was with Dolores, he was everything to me. The sun and moon."

"And after?"

I watched Harvey's pen bob and glide across his notepad.

"I'm not sure."

We looked at each other now, Harvey with his hand poised to continue and I with my mouth closed so that he could not. But the memory held: Dolores standing just behind the man who in my mind was slowly ceasing to be my father; the crowd, humble by comparison to the one that had gathered the year before, when I was still a part of my Source.

Dolores's father had been partial to the demonstrated elegance of zeppelins and had taken us to watch one such flight the month before my extraction in 1906. He was much less enthusiastic about the gliding talents of a fourteen-year-old boy the following summer, but had been swayed to attend by the fact that the young aviator was being called a prodigy and had shared a mentor with the Wright brothers, who'd successfully flown years before. By that and by the fact that his daughter was gaining some notoriety as the Source of the only cognizant Mem to date. That day she and I were to be another attraction of sorts. Before his flight, Dolores posed with the young Laurence Lesh, and after his flight we were all meant to pose together: Dolores, Laurence, myself, and his glider, *Montreal I*.

"I didn't quite understand what had happened until after he was in the water," I began again. Harvey had taken the photograph from my bed while I was distracted and had been staring down at the image of me: head turned on the gurney, eyes too responsive to simply be a shell, a lifeless repository. By the time he looked at me again, his eyes were more responsive, too. They were something different from what they'd been the night we met: unguarded, the way he'd spoken before he remembered I could hear him.

"Who was in the water?" And he smiled when I did.

"I suppose you're no better at reading minds than I am. The boy with the glider. He set a record that day. Twenty-four minutes in the air, ten kilometers above our heads, they said, between the river and the sky. Even my father couldn't pretend not to be impressed." But my smile waned. "Her father."

For a moment it was as though Harvey Parrish were a mirror. His lips fell just as mine had, and when his eyes changed from amusement to something darker, it must also have been because of mine.

"Dolores's father. He whisked her away before she even knew the boy had crashed. Yes, the sky had darkened and heavier clouds had amassed, but the rain was light. No one would have paid it any mind. No one would have needed to be rescued from it. The glide was too eventful, it would seem. Something broke while the Lesh boy was still in the sky, and when they pulled it from the water, his flying machine was destroyed."

"Was he hurt?" he asked, his notepad folded closed.

"Not seriously. But few of us had ever seen a flying machine land, much less crash. There was a commotion and it all became too much."

"But not for you."

"Not for me. Perhaps not for Dolores, if she were ever given the choice." I let my lips lie together before I went too far. "Anyway. That was when the second Mem was born."

Harvey didn't correct my terminology to say that Mems are extracted and not born. He did not wield his pen to transcribe the exchange, and for a moment the room was quiet.

"After that we knew," he said.

I could only nod, suddenly aware of my own breathing.

"She wasn't the special one."

"That's right," I said softly. "Not all of her Mems were like me. It was me, not her. And the papers were no longer interested. Which I suppose is why we made no more appearances together after that summer and why they never called on me again. Her family, that is."

The feeling of loss was something like discomfort; it was a sort of awareness of myself—my breath and my hands—that I did not always possess. But it was more than that as well. Mingled with the unfamiliar self-consciousness was the desire to remain in the moment, to replay it even. To hear him say the words again, despite that they had perhaps only peripherally been about me. The closest facsimile was the experience of watching a romance in the theater, of wishing there were some way to immediately review the most touching moments and title cards.

"But I had a family of my own not long after that. Your father brought me to the Professor's office when Extract No. 2 shared this room with me, and later I met Camille, who took me there again because she didn't know that he and I were already acquainted. They convinced Dolores's father that despite her having less celebrity, I could profit them by mine, if I were free to attend all of the events to which I was invited. They are why I was released from here, my adopted parents and your father, for the time that I was."

My eyes searched the dormitory again, but this time there was not even the memorized vision of cloud and sky. Now the ceiling was pale and close and it was just the Vault. Now the faux stained-glass windows were even more comforting than they'd been the day I'd returned. They interrupted the bland sterility and glowed with colors as rich as mine.

"But he set a record that day," I said. "The Lesh boy. And Dolores doesn't remember."

Dolores Extract No. 2 was what a Mem is meant to be. She was my first real encounter with what I should have been. There was something missing from her eyes, some light or focus, so that even when she was looking at someone it was clear they weren't the true object of her gaze. She could walk and rest and eat—or not—and could be trained to do so to a certain distance or in a certain place or at a certain time, depending on instruction. That was one of two ways in which Mems before me amused society, by having routines imprinted on them despite being otherwise disengaged and unaware of the world around them. The other was the way they could be prompted to recall the memories they housed. Outside responding to that prompting, it was customary that Extract No. 2 spoke infrequently and then only according to the script of that August day in 1907.

"I'm pleased to make your acquaintance," she said to me once, out of the blue.

Little else but Dolores No. 2's unexpected nicety could have pulled me from the first letter of a needlessly lovelorn Fräulein Schmidt. I'd been standing between the beds reading Camille's nearly year-old issue of *The Delineator* aloud. I'd met her only a day or two before and I was still honeymooning over the magazine she'd given me and the stories within. It seemed forever since I'd seen a story acted out—at a party hosted by my mother or one of her friends— and I'd taken to performing them myself. I practiced different accents and affectations, amused by the way the same line could seem to shift meaning depending on my tone.

"What could be more sober?" I'd just asked the otherwise still dormitory, putting effort into making the question seem unanswerable. And then the new Dolores had spoken.

She was not joining my play, though she'd heard it a dozen times in just two days and should've been at wit's end—or would have were she a real person. She was speaking to Laurence Lesh, the boy genius, and for her the Vault was still the riverbank.

I let the magazine close around my finger.

"The pleasure is mine, miss," I said, because he had. She looked at me then, and while I saw my own reflection, to her eyes, memory made me an impressively pensive boy preparing to fly.

I'd never visited with this new Dolores, never asked her where she was from, let alone the question that would prompt her beyond that. I'd been content to spend most of my time elsewhere, taking long constitutionals outside the Vault when it was allowed or visiting the office of the Professor to whom I'd recently been reintroduced. No one seemed to expect how uncomfortable I felt, now that I was not alone in the dormitory, now that there was a memory constantly present, and one I knew well.

I must have done it because of that. To remind myself that she was not mine, this extract who looked exactly like me in the unbecoming gown issued to both of us by the Vault. After all, I'd not lived in the outside world yet; there was nowhere else I felt I belonged. But still. I was certain I did not belong with her.

"Where are you from?" I asked.

Her attention shifted, as it was meant to. At the sound of the question, she engaged, first recalling the date.

"I've just watched a boy fly," she said with a smile. "And what happened today is the most remarkable thing I've ever seen." I was proof that it wasn't—except that by the time Dolores extracted for a second time, she didn't remember the incident we'd seen the year before.

There was a second question, and it would cause a Mem to relay the entirety of their spawning memory. Sometimes it was only the details of whatever event had been extracted; sometimes more: the environment wherever they'd been or thoughts that had occurred to them. It always depended on the Source.

Sitting on the edge of my bed, I took a deep breath before asking, "Dolores Extract No. 2, can you tell me what you dream?"

She did what any Mem would do, what I had learned by observation was expected of me whenever I was asked. First she set the stage. She began with our separate arrivals, the point at which they must have decided the memory began.

"Father and I don't wait long for her to arrive."

There was no point interjecting; the Mem would tell the story her own way, however Dolores recalled it.

"I expect her to look exactly like me, hair and dress included. No one had told me before that I have a Mem of my own, and I half hope that she'll be like a twin, more a sister than a friend. But Father says she'll not be."

She spoke about the river after that, the way it sparkled beneath the summer sun. The way the boy they wanted her to stand beside had at first been less than interested in a budding socialite and her unintentional accomplishment.

"I tell him I haven't done anything, that I know of. Not like him. But he is a sweet child after that, recalling the learned mentor on whose shoulders he is standing and deciding that perhaps we are very much alike."

It was a strange exhilaration, hearing another Mem describe a moment I'd experienced. I'd stood not far from Dolores, watching the exchange while cameras flashed away. I hadn't heard the conversation, but watching my Source and smiling when she smiled kept me from noticing too well the way her father never came over, even after Harvey's father invited him to.

"It is exciting, of course, the motorboat that kites him before he is airborne and gliding on his own. The way I have to tilt my head to see this boy who was so recently standing on the earth, by my side, now soaring in the sky. But my Dolores is more exciting still."

I dared not move. I dared not tempt her to quiet, though I knew she couldn't see me, not really. If she could—if she were the real Dolores—she would've seen that it was me. I was the Mem she spoke of. But of course she was an extract, too, and she was only recalling someone else's memory.

"She keeps watch, even when Laurence is hard to see." Then the Mem laughed. "She's much more Father's daughter than I am, if her shared interest in flight is the judge. Her chaperone hands her a pair of theater glasses which I never see her return. Even when the commotion begins. And I wonder if the way I'm feeling about her is something like a mother hen."

I laughed then at the real Dolores—who I was struggling to remember was not there in the Vault with me—and at myself. All the time she'd been in the Vault with me and I hadn't thought to visit her memory, to see whether I was part of it.

"I tell Father that after today, I think I'd like to see her more."

The quiet that followed was soft. We'd been privy to an exhibit that the city—perhaps the world—would not soon forget. And Dolores, as it turned out, had not paid much mind to what had happened in the sky.

"It was me," I said through a gasp. If Harvey looked alarmed at being jolted out of our shared silence, I didn't see. The room felt empty around me. I was the only one of Dolores's Mems in the world for now; Extract No. 2 was long expired. "She doesn't remember me. He didn't want her to."

By the time I looked at him, Harvey Parrish seemed to understand.

"Dolores doesn't know that I exist."

There was a portrait in the Professor's office in the desk drawer that required a key. The key was affixed to the bottom of the humidor, and the humidor was a plain oak box from the previous century whose interior compartments were lined with a sickly green felt that had been nicked and scratched with use. Along with its first population of cigars, it had been a graduation present. In the years and successes since, the Professor said he'd had far better than those first cigars, but none as satisfying. It was a sentiment about what is treasured that had always distinguished him from my first father, and two years later, when I was recalled to the Vault, I would not forget the conversation we had the day I came into his office to find him staring into that drawer.

"The greatest inventions are not born of necessity or genius," he said. "They are born of pain."

He withdrew a thick black card, the portrait held inside by sliding its corners into slits made in the parchment. At first he studied it without moving, and I held my breath to keep from disrupting him.

"Or perhaps that's only true of mine." He approached my seat then, and in his hands he held the card closed, pressing it between his forefingers and thumbs as though to make a border from the impressions.

I offered my hand when he seemed hesitant, but instead of extending the card, the Professor bent before me.

"You are a miracle, ma petite, and nothing will change that. It is I who am not what I appear. And I wanted you to know."

The story, as a real person might say, was in the picture, but the picture alone could not have told it, so he waited while I opened the card and saw for the first time what had been his inspiration.

A baby girl lay posed in a bassinette, half her body propped up on a generous pillow. She was dressed in a beautiful nightgown, long enough to conceal her legs and feet. I couldn't be sure how old she was in days or weeks, as her size was dwarfed by her surroundings, but judging by the sparseness of her fine hair, I thought she must be newly born. Her eyes were closed, her hands lying peacefully over her abdomen. She could have been a doll, but for one certainty.

"This child is dead."

The Professor nodded and took back the card, closing it and turning again toward the open drawer.

"Did she belong to you?"

"Camille and I," he said, before looking at me with a smile from some other time. "But she belonged more to Camille, I think. I remember thinking that she would have loved me, in time, because of how her mother did. And though I never got to see it, I will always be grateful to Cam for that."

The drawer was locked and the key returned to the bottom of the humidor.

"I couldn't let her fade away," he said of his wife. "When I lost hope that she could live with the loss, I began to wonder whether she could forget, whether I could help her to."

From there, I knew the rest. The wonderings of a brilliant man had already yielded so great a number of impossible feats, to the good of friends and strangers alike. The Professor had set to work devising a way to spare his wife the memory of her child. And the fact that I was there, listening to the story, meant he had succeeded.

"Where are her Mems?"

A spitting sound crowded the end of my query and his shoulders quaked. To account for the quantity of his sudden tears I thought the Professor would have needed another pair of eyes. It was a heart-wrenching scene. By 1923 I'd lived in the outside world for a number of years and had begun to feel more than my own emotions. I found myself empathizing with characters on film even though I well knew they weren't real people, and the Professor meant so much more than they did. I'd come to love him in place of the father who didn't rightfully belong to any Dolores but the Source—and whose convictions meant only one Dolores could ever be his daughter. I adored him in place of the first Banker Parrish, who may have loved me back but, once I was released, seemed content enough with the memory of me. At the sight of the Professor's uncharacteristic unraveling, I rushed to his side, wrapping my arms about him. That my question had incited such an outburst only concerned me more.

"That, I could not bear," he said when he could speak, his arms around my waist as I swayed us both. "It was the worst of Camille, the darkest bit of despair."

"There was only one?"

"Only one procedure, ma petite, you must understand. I took all of the pregnancy in one extraction. Everything, and everything it touched. Pieces of us, of conversations and parties. Times I would like to have kept. I had to be sure she'd be completely free."

I couldn't speak, the weight and breadth of what he described becoming increasingly clear. By all rights, there should have been hundreds of Mems, thousands perhaps, to account for every moment or event that Camille had experienced during pregnancy. In some ways, it must have been easier to take what amounted to nearly a year of her life than to individually find them all.

"It wasn't enough for Camille to forget," I said when the second realization overwhelmed me. "What about her friends and family, surely they would have known?"

"They wanted her well as much as I did," he answered. "Her family said she was the luckiest wife." He almost spat the words. "She'd married the only man who could spare her such pain."

I thought of my own parents and the secrets they'd agreed to keep from Dolores the moment they rushed her to the clinic, the things they vowed never to discuss after her extractions, though she'd never remember them now. It seemed a sacrifice any number of families would make, and I couldn't imagine they would lament escaping the memory themselves. The grand charade was never just for the Source.

"What happened to the Mem?" I asked.

The Professor had held me all this time, but now he released me and stood, taking a step back in case I didn't want to be near when he answered. "I stayed with her until she expired, but I helped her to go quickly. It was painless. But for the prick of the syringe, she felt nothing, I can promise you that."

My eyes grew wide and he took me by the shoulders.

"And you must never speak a word of it to Camille, if you love her. Of how this all began. She doesn't know she was the first."

"She doesn't know she had a procedure?"

"She didn't know anything about my research, about the technology I was creating, or that it was for her. Don't you understand, I wanted her whole again and happy."

"And what about you?"

As the words escaped me, I wondered whether my tone was curious or condemning. We'd spoken about Mems a thousand times, clinically discussing their short lives and the way they both existed and did not. And though they resembled someone with a life and a light inside them, Mems were something akin to shells, keepsake boxes housing memories sometimes precious but often despised. I should feel nothing at the news that my Professor had helped one to expire when she would have anyway. It shouldn't require every ounce of restraint to keep my mind from wandering into labyrinths. Whether Camille Extract No. 1 had been exceptional was too bizarre to consider when my mind still caught on the fact that there'd been one in the first place.

I said it again in my head.

Camille Extract No. 1.

How long would she have lasted with so extensive a spawning memory? Might the first of our kind have been like me? Had being extracted by the man involved in her memory had any effect? To imagine him destroying her without first investigating the countless possibilities, without allowing his staff—hand-selected for their passion—to study the only Mem related to the father of extraction science, added a horrible weight to his confession. Each time I thought my mind had exhausted the questions, there came another. Because knowing him as I did, as a loving man without prejudice, I could not help imagining what he must have said—and I could not imagine a scenario in which he hadn't spoken—while she died.

I studied him: his face and countenance; his posture. I waited, half expecting him to change, to shift before my very eyes as he certainly must now.

"Were you happy when it was done?" I asked. "Are you now?"

"I was as happy as I could be." His heavy hands slid down my arms and away, whatever reservation I tried to contain falling as well.

It occurred to me in that moment that I would have to choose to keep him as the Professor I knew and understood. That I could. Because his confession was not solely born of immodesty, out of a desire to be taken from his pedestal; he had carried this secret for years, first taking it from his wife and then having to keep it from her. Unlike the others who knew, he was with Camille every day. The hope she'd lost had been his, too. He hadn't extracted the memories of their dead child from himself, nor had he extracted the memory of silencing her Mem. He kept a portrait of what began it in a locked place, preserved for stolen glances. I was hearing all of this to share his burden. To be his confidante. An honor that none but he and Camille had thought me worthy.

"At least," I began, nodding my eventual certainty before the sentence was spoken, "your work has done what you intended it to. You've spared Camille and others the hurt that might have killed them."

His chest expanded as though I'd breathed into him. Resuscitated for the moment, only later would he confess that his work had done much more. To be sure, I hadn't known Camille before the procedure. The absentmindedness that had been so endearing, and by no means abnormal, was now an alarming indication of the procedure's effect. I remembered: Camille losing track of time; Camille misplacing a teaspoon though she still held it in her hand; Camille missing the trolley stop she'd used for ages. It turned out these were all a very small price to pay for extracting ten months of her life in one sitting, but it was a first glimpse of what—in other patients—would be called a fractured or fragmented mind.

The next time I sat in the Professor's office, there was a man with us whose price had been markedly higher. If Camille was pleasantly absentminded, Walter Gordon was so distractible as to appear simple. He'd been meeting with the Professor for several years by the time I observed one of his sessions, and though I occupied a visible seat in the corner, the man said to have eyes all over Chicago never noticed me.

He was the typical portrait of the kind of man who patronized the Professor's clinic. It wasn't love or death and it was rarely betrayal that sent them there. While women came desiring any number of memories extracted and for a variety of reasons, it seemed that men had an almost singular experience with which they couldn't make peace.

He'd *earned* their removal, Walter told the Professor. He'd made a name for himself—though he had to share it with his father—and he'd told himself that only when his fortune was made did he deserve to be rid of the ugly past that chased him there.

It wasn't the memory of his father's swift hand he needed to forget. Not exactly. It was the humiliation of being hit, of flinching and drawing back, of being a small boy in the first place. Of being helpless, or at least of thinking he'd been. But when those memories were gone, it seemed the humiliation stayed behind, infecting other memories that had at first seemed more benign.

The first Walter Mems never lived longer than a year. They were little boys afraid of the daylight. When they left the corners of their dormitory, they scurried around the facility like beaten dogs, except that their heads stayed tucked between their shoulders like little turtles. In their nervous condition, they sometimes ran into doors or the corners of walls despite having been trained safe routes to wander. And even though Walter never spared a thought to how they were faring or that they were in the Vault in the first place, it was for Mems such as Walter's that the Professor brought nurses into the facility. Mems were personal possessions and, like a bank, the Vault strived to foster confidence that nothing but expiration would alter a Source's belonging.

At first it seemed an overreaction. The young Walter Mems were the only extracts to that point to suffer injury, and theirs were thankfully slight and unintentional. Mems, after all, did not respond to their environments. While Bankers had noticed infrequent examples of Mems seeming to interact with their surroundings, it was clear that they perceived those surroundings as aspects of the memories they housed, not as they truly were. The young Walters who scurried fled from their father, not the Bankers, no matter how it looked to visitors.

If a Banker or able-bodied student could not easily restrain the young ones, there was nothing the new wave of nurses could possibly have done with Walter Gordon's later Mems—the ones from his teenage years, when he'd gotten old enough to answer evil with evil, when he'd gotten strong enough to hit his father back. The memories had been anger once, or even pride—after all, he'd been the victor in the matches against his erstwhile Goliath almost as often as not. Those memories motivated him to prove his father wrong, to excel in his studies and then in the more profitable extracurriculars, to make every self-earned cent count. The fistfights and cauliflower ears meant he could do anything, that he could live on scraps while he magpied for the future. Now, in the years of hard-won excess, they were embarrassment; they were embittered and enraged at being controlled, at looking anything like Walter Sr. Those Mems were festering and dangerous. At first, it seemed they could not possibly last, and then it seemed they hung on out of defiance, refusing to expire. While the younger Walters had shrunk a little each day, a disquieting mélange of terror and surprise contorting their mouths even after their final breaths, the older ones stepped out of shadows, frightening the receptionists and staff. They curled forward, walking hunched and always baring their teeth. And without them—the young and the older—Walter Gordon was slowly slipping away.

"Walter," the Professor said, craning his neck in an attempt to catch the man's drifting eye. "Let's stay on task, shall we?"

He was gentle, with what seemed like limitless patience. The Professor often reduced it to professionalism, but I had seen Bankers fray. Even when they didn't unravel completely, it was often not without discernible effort and necessary breaks. The Professor's compassion was genuine. Their conditions, after all, were his doing.

"Wally? Can you tell me what you had for breakfast this morning?"

"Eggs," Walter answered, adjusting in his seat and trying with all his might to keep from investigating the many weights and knickknacks on the desk between them.

"Eggs." The Professor read the notes provided by Walter's maid. "Yes, that's right. And how were they prepared?"

"I know this." Only he wasn't responding to the question, but rather to the inkwell before him.

"Indeed, you do. You've been here many times. In a moment, you'll get to tell me everything you remember from my desk, every scratch. But for the time being, I'd like to know how your eggs were prepared this morning. Can you tell me that?"

"Yes, they were hard. Lydia used a spoon to break the shell for me."

The Professor smiled and made an annotation on the paper. Frankly, the sight of a grown man behaving in such a way was hardly a smiling matter. It defied everything I knew, and I felt sick in Walter's presence.

In the sitting room, a Banker and nurse observed a fractured Source, on holiday from both her native Paris and her senses, with one of her Mems. Alongside a dozen other sights, it was one I would never have seen in the year after I was born, back before the staff knew of fragmenting minds or had entertained the notion that extracted memories might help in their treatment. Nevertheless, there they were: the Source wearing a sloppy frock that the nurse had given up trying to keep on both the woman's shoulders, and the Mem wearing exactly what is required in the Vault and looking remarkably more put together as a result.

No questions were asked; no attempts made to guide the visit. The Banker and nurse simply sat the two together and kept them there, hoping for something to happen, something that science had yet to identify, which might benefit the woman who'd given too much of herself away. Inside the Vault, everything was an experiment.

"It's not as though she can reabsorb her memory," I said to Harvey when he found me observing the scene. "How can sitting beside her Mem help?"

"It's your fault, to be honest." He was eating a small helping of ice cream from a paper bowl.

"Mine?"

"Mm-hmm. You so damaged our intellectual hubris that we'll try almost anything now, we're so completely at a loss for an explanation."

I couldn't decide whether to laugh. It was one of those strange remarks offered in jest that nevertheless displays all the hallmarks of honesty. I hadn't known till then that my condition could be thought costly if it meant men of science must confess their limitations.

"Is that chocolate?" I asked instead.

He looked surprised but handed me the dish. "I suppose you even have a favorite meal."

"I don't see how anyone could. Some things I love because the smell reminds me of my childhood, and then there are the things I like most when I'm sad or happy. And I love the popcorn from my movie theater better than all the other theaters in town. I could never choose a favorite food."

When I turned to gauge his response, he was moving his jaw as though nibbling bits of something more substantial than ice cream.

"Is that strange?"

"No," he said. "Not for a person. Or a Mem like you."

He was still standing a bit behind my chair when he reached around and collected the now empty dish. In what could have been an experiment of my own, I considered too late what he may have done if I'd left a bite for him in the paper bowl. Clearly he'd been intrigued to share food with a Mem when he offered it to me, but would he have eaten again after I was done? And then the thoughts muddled, a wave of cologne reaching around me along with the shadow he cast.

"Anyway, I hope all this isn't a complete waste of time," he said, nodding toward the scene when he returned from the trash bin. "I'd like to think fractured Sources can be rehabilitated somehow."

"Perhaps if the law were written more clearly, they wouldn't be fractured in the first place."

"But even better if the procedure could be perfected."

I'd never felt such a rush of violent disagreement. It rolled up the length of my torso and burned my chest, as if more than a mere opinion. It was strong enough in fact that suppressing it took effort.

"If people are imperfect enough to destroy their minds, perhaps they cannot perfect the procedure that allows them to do so."

Harvey dismissed my logic. "That's rather literal. It's more a matter of scientific integrity. Regardless the invention in question, regardless what it does—if we've created it, we must strive to perfect it, if we can."

I nodded, but my mind was unchanged. In place of challenging the sentiment, I turned my attention to a more selfish concern. I was, after all, a creation. Other Mems didn't perceive the world outside the memories they housed, but did my being an exception and garnering the attention of scientists and socialites alike make me any less imperfect?

Harvey had wandered closer to the observing Banker, crossing his arms over his chest and cinching his eyebrows as he stared at the static scene. The Mem hiccupped a smile every now and again, her head pulling back a bit and her shoulders hopping. The Source failed to notice her spawn, eventually drifting into a light sleep that was interrupted by the slightest sound. Even a layperson could see the futility of this pairing, and still Harvey looked on, engrossed.

I rose without scratching the floor with my chair—so as not to wake the fractured woman—and en route to my dormitory, I heard a familiar radio show before I arrived at the nurses' station. I hesitated in the hall. The station wasn't visible from where I stood; I could not see the nurse but I knew it was the one I'd upset. In the weeks since my arrival, she'd feigned obliviousness each time we crossed paths. And then, before I knew what I was doing, I approached her again. She could hardly pretend not to see me when I folded my arms on the countertop and leaned forward to look at the radio, but even when her mouth fell open, she said nothing.

"Hello," I said anyway. "How are you?"

"I'm well." She leaned all the way back in her chair but didn't appear any more relaxed.

"I don't particularly like the way you seem to recoil from me, being so thoroughly convinced as I am that I've never done you any harm. But, if you don't object, I'd like to forgive you your insensitivity. I forgive everyone else's, after all."

For a moment the radio program filled in the space between us. Having not planned out the confrontation ahead of time, I decided I would simply remain with my arms folded on the countertop, enjoying the rest of the broadcast, should she refuse to talk to me. But she didn't.

"I suppose I do owe you an apology," she admitted quietly. "My awe should have worn off by now, shouldn't it?"

"What is it about me that has you so perplexed?" I asked.

"I'm not sure exactly. Mostly the way you carry yourself. The same thing that fascinates everyone else, I guess. But it was silly of me not to get past it."

"Curious. As far as I can tell, I've been walking on eggshells for the last couple of weeks. I don't feel fascinating; I feel as though I might never regain my bearings."

"Well now," she said, leaning forward to fold her own arms on the desk below the countertop, the starch in her posture gone. "That makes two of us."

No. 5

In my time in the real world, Camille and the Professor had been my closest friends, though they were more like parental figures than intimates. While they were supportive of my striking up friendships, I hesitated to grow too familiar, fearing that they would be too superficial to be satisfying. This hypothesis was not disproved when tested. On the rare occasion that I did reveal my identity, I found that my new acquaintances either admitted that they'd known all along, in which case they proved impossible to trust, or they would become immediately more attentive, inviting me out and introducing me around so often that I was quite obviously on display.

It would've been impossible to maintain the friends I had in 1906—the ones I grew up with, who debuted with me and those I made after. They still had Dolores for one thing, and for another, I was not the girl I'd been before extraction. Setting aside the confusion of having two identical friends—and what I assumed would be an inevitably constant comparison in which I could never be thought original—I was certain that despite my ladylike hobbies of mah-jongg and theatergoing, my long-lost girlfriends wouldn't have approved of my familiarity with gentlemen's business: the ongoing research studies taking place in the Vault and in the Professor's office; the matters involving the board, which sometimes kept the Professor up late into the night. And if those things weren't bad enough, they certainly wouldn't have thought it good practice to be too often in the company of a single girl, as I assumed they were long since married by now.

And so the weeks that passed before Camille was to visit me in the Vault would have been unbearably lonesome if not for the new nurse. Her name was Étienne, after her father, she said, but the name embarrassed her and she preferred Ettie instead.

"You smoke?" I asked when I spotted her retrieving a white pack of Marlboros from her pocket. It was early evening, and we were standing in the courtyard above the Vault.

"I am a mild, respectable woman, after all," she said with a wink.

I declined when she offered one to me.

"I won't finish it or we'll miss the start of the program," she said, but then took a long drag and blew the smoke above our heads into the fading light.

September 20, 1925, had at once come quickly and also seemed to take its time. Recently, CKAC had begun airing an instructional series on playing piano, and part of me had truly believed I'd be released and back at home by the time it began, learning along with scores of listeners on my neighbor's piano. But that was before I knew of reprinting and that I'd been recalled so that I could be erased. Now I swayed between hoping that my fate would change and despairing that, at least for me, piano lessons would soon be obsolete.

"Today makes three weeks exactly," I said.

Ettie held the cigarette between her fingers and rubbed her bottom lip for stray paper with the same hand. I tried not to watch too intently so that she wouldn't see my disapproval. It had nothing to do with her being a woman, of course; rather I was cautious over the safety of a practice whose advertised purpose had changed too many times. Real people, it seemed, were less skeptical. They appeared always too trusting of easy pleasures.

"Three weeks, that's right," Ettie said with a nod. "For the both of us. The day you returned was my first night on staff, did you know?" And then she laughed. "You could tell, of course you could."

She passed her cigarette to me absentmindedly and I pinched it between my fingers as she had.

"What made you come belowground?"

"Nothing complicated or noble, I promise. I've always wanted a Mem of my own, and Vault nurse and staff benefits include discounted extractions after six months in Vault employ. Well, on one extraction anyway, and one is all I need."

"Then there's something you'd like to forget?" I asked as gently as I could without insulting her. Ettie and I had agreed that when it was just she and I we needn't coddle each other's feelings the way men often did.

"No, nothing like that," she said, but took a moment longer before she continued. "I just wanted to know how it felt to have one. A Mem. But more than that, the experience. What's it like to know there's something you'll never remember?" She scoffed at her own question. "Silly!"

It brought to mind a question the Professor had asked me a number of months before and how—had I responded differently—I would have been able to provide Ettie with an answer to her own.

"Is that so silly?" I asked.

"It is now that I know you. Now that I know the Mem I'd extract might be more. It feels downright selfish to me. Curiosity doesn't seem reason enough."

"No," I said, balancing myself between a memory and the present. "It doesn't." I looked at my friend. "But you're being hard on yourself. It's more likely your Mem would be a keepsake, like all the others."

"In that case, it's just cruel. Trapping one moment or feeling inside someone and then leaving them to expire when the feeling runs its course."

Ettie had taken back her cigarette and quickly inhaled from it a few times before stamping it out.

"Come on. We'll be late for the show."

Once the program ended, I returned to my dormitory. Ettie would go home in the morning, not to return for three full days. But Camille would soon be here and she was dotingly maternal in a way Ettie wasn't. In fact, she would be here in the morning, and I couldn't decipher precisely why thinking of one should make me think about the other—perhaps a Mem like me had capacity enough for only so much affection. Perhaps I had a finite capacity for friendships that confirmed our shared identity and that would offend real people if they could hear my thoughts. I tried to settle my restless mind with endless logical explanations and hypotheses but only succeeded in keeping myself awake. So I withdrew from the world around me, from the sterility of the Vault where smells lacked texture and every sound was hollow. I comforted myself by remembering the carol of the city streets and the collective laughter one both hears and feels burrowed deep in the cocoon of a theater's plush seats. I remembered the world I'd honestly believed was my home and the way I'd enjoyed observing the endless varieties of real people.

It was Walter Gordon, his hunched figure crowding my doorframe, that brought me back to the Vault. My shoulder crashed into the headboard at the sight of him, my back climbing the hard wood as I quickly sat up. Even the hall light seemed terrified, trembling behind the young man, the false moonlight from my artificial windows falling between us so that I couldn't make out his face.

"You thought you were different, didn't you?" In the darkness, his voice was rough as gravel and it rumbled low in the space between us. Walter Gordon stepped into the room and a chill blossomed under the perspiration already beading my forehead and collarbone.

"What do you want?"

Had they not already evaporated in the still air, my words would have turned tail and hurried back to me at the sound of his growl. He took two long strides to the center of my room and I let out something resembling a horse's whinny.

"Walter, stop!" I cried, though the helplessness I felt seemed confirmation that he wouldn't.

When he reached my bed, Walter's Mem sat beside me, his eyes boring into mine and his hands pressing into the board on either side of my head so that I was penned in.

"You thought you were different, didn't you?" he asked again, and I shook my head. The stained-glass light washed his face now, his teeth glistening in a frightening smirk, and a knot tightened in my stomach.

"Where are you from?" I asked to disrupt whatever he was a memory of. The question would draw him out, at least momentarily. He wasn't addressing me, I knew that. It wasn't me he was seeing. There was nothing but happenstance to account for the fact that he'd stopped at my dormitory, no reason but chance that he'd spoken those words to me in particular, and still I recoiled from his accusation.

"Where are you from?" I demanded again.

In the next moment, Walter was struggling to breathe. His shoulders heaved, puffs of his breath breaking against my skin. There was something feral about the sounds coming from him. I feared he would open his mouth and an unearthly beast would claw its way out. And then—finally and because he had no choice—he answered.

"September 20, 1915. I'm standing at the mirror, but I recently stood above my father's bloody body. I could have killed him this time and I'm not sure I didn't."

"It isn't 1915 anymore, Walter," I said, flinching and turning my head each time he snarled. "This is 1925 and you didn't kill your father."

Before I can explain the Vault and the memories, and without rearing back, a young Walter Gordon slams his forehead into mine.

I am the mirror before him and I shatter into pieces.

The memory comes though I'm not asleep. I am unconscious and so the record begins.

I am the as yet unreplicated Dolores, young and complete and wearing a fashionable capelet over my corseted dress with elbow-length powder-blue gloves that match my dress and capelet exactly. My long copper hair is rolled and pinned a thousand times to climb above my head like a halo, roses woven in. It is August 11, 1906. It's been less than a year since I began dressing like a debuted woman and I still feel as though I'm in a glamorous parade each time I take to the city streets.

I am accompanying my parents to brunch, where an impressive young man will join us. This one is in town for little more than a day and, like the others I've met so far who live outside Montreal and therefore haven't been introduced at some social event, I am the reason he's here. My parents and I have taken a coach far from Centre-Ville and we've only just disembarked when it happens.

I think I hear the woman's screams before the collision, but I know that can't be right. It isn't a matter of my being nineteen and freshly debuted; few people in this city have ever encountered an automobile accident and it's only natural that I understand the woman's sounds first. It is anguish, a tearing as of something delicate and sacred. It is a moment that divides her life into the time before this tragedy and the time after.

When I turn to face the chaotic scene, men are hustling in seemingly every direction and their purpose is unclear. Someone, a stranger turned guardian, turns the woman from the sight and holds her to his chest. Others stand in the intersection, keeping the offending motorist from leaving the scene, and still others begin to huddle around the broken body of the victim. In their midst there is a very young girl, forgotten in the madness. She stares down at the mangled body of her father and, for a few crucial seconds, no one thinks to obstruct her view.

The smell is thick and alarming, wafting to our side of the intersection as if in a hurry to spread. If the smoke and sizzle are any indication, it will linger a long while. The fragrance of roasting meat is the final insult, stealing what remains of the fallen man's dignity. It isn't a charred smell, as when a fire cooks too quickly, but a savory musk. An ordinary and enticing aroma that means the automobile must have branded him through his clothes and that his flesh still cooks.

Together with the endless stare of his daughter, the almost sweet smell of the man's flesh sends me into hysterics. This moment is the first of its kind in Montreal, and so is the dead man. On all sides of the accident, pedestrians, streetcar patrons, and motorists alike vacillate between hysteria and calm. There is no way to know which will become the standard response when automobile accidents become commonplace.

But there is something else. An understanding that this is possible. It is possible to be killed by the most prized of possessions, to be destroyed by the greatest invention of our time. It is possible to die in the street no matter how you began the day. This is the first universal truth I have ever come by on my own and it multiplies like fire. Because if this is possible—if sudden death is no respecter of persons—so must every horrid thing be.

The stench slips between my father's arms and finds me, and when I beg my father to make it go away, the smoke leaps into my mouth, masking my voice with a foreign rasp. He hushes me, careful with my hair and flowers, and promises it will be all right as he hurries my mother and me inside. I cannot make such a public scene, he whispers, but I feel incapable of calm. I am changed, I want to tell him.

By now my father is speaking more to my mother than to me, charging her to remind me of proper conduct. It's no use. A chasm exists between us that never has before.

I know something they do not. Together we witnessed a moment that only I seem to understand.

Like Montreal, I will never be the same.

Camille's voice gave me the courage to open my eyes.

At first consciousness approached and then retreated again, ebbing like an evening tide that prefers the inseparable darkness where the water meets the sky. Somewhere between the end and beginning of the memory, I sensed the Vault building up around me, and when it didn't insist—when the bright day began again instead and our coach stopped outside the restaurant—I was relieved not to face Walter Gordon again. Only when I heard Camille was I safe, no longer afraid that to wake would be to find the violent Mem still on my bed.

I flinched at the light. Camille's ample figure was warped and hazy, the remnants of my ordeal giving her usually comforting image a nightmarish undertone that I could not have described.

"Oh, Dolores, Dolores," she said through a relieved gasp, falling over me and then drawing us both upright.

Each time she squeezed, I felt as though a long crack was splitting my forehead in two. Lifting the hand not trapped between us, I let my fingertips graze my brow. There they met a starchy bandage that wrapped entirely around my head, the place where Walter had made contact protruding against it.

"What has that animal done to you, Dolores?"

The crack split further still. Her embrace was not to blame. It was the name intensifying the pain and panic, both at the site of the wound and inside my head; I pulled myself away.

"Dolores? Dolores, what's the matter?"

As I threw back the covers and prepared to stand at the bedside opposite her, Camille hurried into the hall to call for help, her heels skittering across the linoleum. She came quickly back, begging me to lie down or at least tell her what was the matter. The sound of the splitting seemed to forbid my answering her. If only I could get through the haze, I knew that I could set things right.

I made my way to the armoire by imagining the robe, the way the silk would feel against my bare arms. It might still smell of my flat and the entrancing incense I'd found on Dorchester Boulevard one afternoon, the thin coil of smoke drawing me like a pied piper into the shop I would frequent after that first intoxication. As my head shot through with a piercing pain and I thought my knees might give, I held the memories of my home and my freedom at the forefront of my mind, like a carrot dangling before an otherwise immobile mule. Slowly, I progressed.

By the time Harvey arrived, I'd withdrawn my Elsie robe and slung it across my shoulders, working in one arm with stiff apprehension. Camille stood frozen in distress, cupping her mouth with one hand and separating he and I, until Harvey finally stepped around her and helped me finish dressing myself. I closed the armoire's long doors and held myself there for a moment, breathing deeply while I let it support my weight.

"That's all she wanted," Harvey said to Camille without turning around. "No harm done."

"But let's get her back in bed at once," she said, the directive giving Harvey permission to take me by the hand and shoulder and return me there. "I was afraid she'd grow faint and hurt herself. You could've given me some warning, Dolores." Her laugh was forced and hopeful, even as I winced at the name again, but at least the splitting was done.

"I'm sorry." I took her hand after Harvey moved away. It was easy to smile now and surprisingly easier to cry, but I would not allow myself. It was our first reunion and Camille had already been upset.

"No," she said. "It's me who's sorry. I knew this place was wrong for you. I should've..." The words or the intention gathered too quickly in her throat and she struggled to express them. "...done something more. I should've insisted we keep you out of here."

"You couldn't have, Madame Toutant."

Harvey was right, but Camille shook her head anyway. With each moment that she didn't speak, the horizon of tears in her eyes swelled higher and higher.

"It isn't fair." Her shoulders fell forward then, tiny droplets sprinkling our entwined hands. "You've no idea what she's like, Dolores. She isn't fit to decide what becomes of you."

My stomach somersaulted.

"What is she like?" I managed to ask, but Camille hadn't known the real Walter Gordon. She hadn't known any of the clients I'd observed with the Professor. She'd no idea that I truly wanted to know—not what she thought of my Source, but what my Source had become.

"She's a horrible mess, like the rest of them, populating this Vault with frightened or frightening Mems who can't be trusted and then forgetting about them. And that's the point, isn't it?" she scoffed. "To be rid of them even if the world isn't. Sometimes I wish he'd never begun any of this."

When I caught her eye, she smiled through her ribbons of tears and held my face in one of her clammy hands. In her sigh was a conclusion, like a mother who has been overwhelmed in front of her child and then calms herself, for their sake. That she had been a mother and couldn't remember made the affection all the more wrenching.

"But he'll put it right." She nodded as though I'd insisted. "He won't let her back inside without a fight."

"What do you mean?"

"The Professor is seeking an injunction on the basis of Dolores's impaired mental state, to keep her from extracting any more memories," Harvey explained. He stood beside my bed, his hands behind his back, his posture more resembling a guard than a Banker.

Camille gave an exasperated exhale and chuckled, taking my hand again. "Courtrooms and injunctions and attorneys. It'll be the death of him. He's in the courthouse as much as he's on campus these days."

"Why is he there so often?" I asked, unsure whether to be pleased with such efforts on my behalf or whether to be ashamed of what I was costing him.

"Oh, if it isn't what's to be done with those awful, angry Mems, it's the Dowager Keepsakes." She waved her hand above her head as though dispersing a cloud of Ettie's smoke, and I wished Harvey had been anywhere but close enough to hear. The walls of my dormitory would have laughed at me for thinking all the Professor's fight was for my benefit. "It's always something, isn't it?"

Before I could ask anything more, Harvey stepped closer and my voice evaporated.

"For now, Walter Extract No. 17 is confined to his dormitory," he said. "You won't see him again."

"Oh, Dolores, I'm so glad you're all right." Camille laid her head against my chest, covering my monogram, and I pressed my cheek into her soft hair.

"I am, I promise. And now you've worn yourself out. Please go home and rest."

"I couldn't."

"I'm all right now," I insisted. I could not consider everything I'd heard and maintain the appropriate levity to keep Camille's worries at bay, nor would Harvey speak freely in her presence. "We'll visit again."

When she finally agreed to go, it was without telling me when she would be back or when the Professor intended to visit. It stung to know that though leaving me there was hard, it was also a relief. But I could hardly blame her. There was no reason for us both to suffer simply because I had no choice. To be honest, now that I'd seen her I worried it would be harder living inside the Vault than before she'd come.

Harvey returned after showing Camille out but made no effort to speak with me. Without warning or apparent consideration, he began to dress my wound, his face tense with concentration. Even when I winced, he was undeterred, breaking from his trance only when I physically moved his hand away from me.

"That hurts."

"Oh." He drew a breath in through his nose and let his hands fall into his lap with the fresh bandage and ointment. "The skin is broken."

"Then take care with it." I said, turning slightly away. "Do other Mems really not feel pain? Not even the Walters or Keepsakes?"

"Not in my experience, no. Unless it's part of the memory."

"Well, I do." When he didn't cease staring at my injury, I gathered my courage and leaned forward, nevertheless flinching when he resumed. "Gently, please."

And when he dabbed the splintered skin with ointment, the difference in his touch was startling. Either he was different or I was, and the latter was the only reasonable explanation. He was not the one who seemed to change based on the setting and company. Only I could have been at first something inanimate and then, in the space of a minute, become a girl with whom one must be delicate.

"Would an injunction really stop Dolores from having any more procedures?" I asked when he was beginning to wind the new bandage around my head.

"At least until further considerations were made."

In my mind, I replaced Harvey's sterile definition with a more optimistic conclusion: "So it would keep her from reprinting me."

"Until the court resolved whether or not she is of sound mind to oversee her property."

Of course outside the Vault, the concern would have to prove more encompassing than the status of a single Mem. By property, they meant everything from Dolores's family's estate—whatever else she'd amassed in the nineteen years since we'd been apart.

"Does she have much property?"

Harvey focused his attention on the pad he'd retrieved from the breast pocket of his lab coat, flipping back and forth between pages while he spoke.

"Jointly, with her husband, she has the home in West Island, but that wouldn't be considered. I assume he's the primary signatory. On her own, she has a portion of her father's estate and portfolio, which ironically involves the board of directors for this clinic, though he shifted to emeritus status a year or so ago."

"Her husband?"

Now he glanced up at me. My heart skipped a beat.

"Did I—did she marry him?"

"Did she marry whom?"

I didn't remember his first name, not at first. Of course it was impossible for me to remember any part of Dolores's life after the accident—whether my father had carried on with our brunches or whether we'd proceeded immediately to the clinic, though the latter seemed too sensational to be discreet.

"Shepherd," I said at last. "A Mr. Shepherd."

"Mr. Lyman Shepherd," he confirmed with a nod as he replaced the notepad in his pocket. "Indeed she did."

Now he stood, his fingers lacing behind him and his gaze surveying the room once more so that I knew he meant to leave.

"Wait. Don't go."

He stopped as though we were children playing 'Jean Dit.' As though he were under some enchantment that kept him there but did not require that he turn from the door.

"Not just yet," I added, closing my eyes as if to seal myself up and breathing again only when I heard him reclaim his seat before me.

"Was it well attended?" I asked, though I didn't care. I tried to imagine planning the wedding with my mother and Lyman's—whomever she was—but could conjure only flickering pictures from a movie screen or portraits of brides in magazines. None of it calmed me or hinted at whether it was Walter's attack, the Vault walls, or something else that made me feel so strange.

"It certainly looked that way to me," Harvey said, and my interest was piqued.

"You were there?"

"I was. But I'm afraid I won't be of much use describing the gown or the flowers or the way you wore your hair." He cleared his throat. "The way Dolores wore it." He adjusted in his chair and recrossed his legs. "I was a child when she was married, barely eight years old."

For some reason, the thought made me smile. A child-sized Harvey. A little boy in a child-sized lab coat with pale eyes and a stern expression.

When I laughed out loud, a flicker of a smile surfaced on his lips but didn't bloom.

"Is that funny?"

I imagined my child-sized Harvey with a man-sized head, and I laughed so hard I lost my breath. I let my head fall back against the headboard, though the motion and the amusement sent a succession of throbbing stabs through it. Finally, I forced myself to settle for fear that the pain would break the seal and saturate my new bandage with fresh blood.

"Were you the same back then?" I asked, struggling to catch my breath.

"I don't suppose so." He seemed to know now that my laughter had been at his expense. "I wasn't a serious child, if that's what you mean."

I drew my lips into my mouth to keep them from smiling or suggesting that his reckoning was too biased to be believed.

"My father saw to it that I had a childhood, no matter how hard he worked." When he spoke of his father, Harvey relaxed at the edges. "Serious matters were for later in life, he always said."

"What a relief to finally be an adult then," I said with a smile. "Free to be serious about everything, all the time. No one to insist upon balance."

I don't know why I thought he would smile at that, and he certainly wouldn't laugh. I'd never seen or heard him do so. I had no idea how to inspire him to either. There was only the subject of science that obviously and consistently engaged him.

"Have you ever had the procedure, Harvey? Have you ever extracted a Mem?"

As though perpetually drawn from a maze of deep and encompassing thoughts, Harvey first cleared his throat and then adjusted in his seat again.

"My father was against it. For me, at least. He was entirely enamored of its study. But he would never have let me or my mother take part, not in that way. He said there were too many outcomes impossible to foresee."

"You were a lucky child."

"Yes," he said, looking delicately at me. "I was."

His eyes softened the longer we watched each other so that I couldn't bring myself to discuss my own father, whose affection I knew I'd have to remand to the real Dolores. If I did I would also have to confess knowing that his love did not extend to an extract, and so perhaps my opinion of how he treated Dolores was moot. If his real daughter thought him protective and wise, what did it matter that I was offended on her behalf? He hadn't trusted her to manage the pain of having witnessed the accident or else, given her recent debut and courting season, he hadn't thought it worthwhile to allow her the chance. The consequences from which Harvey's father had wisely shielded his son were either beyond Dolores's father or unimportant.

In the end I said nothing, unwilling to disrupt our comfortable silence even to tell Harvey what my spawning memory had taught me of the world, its fragility and the brief nature of its favor. This knowledge was uniquely mine. It had been extracted with Dolores's memory of witnessing the death of the first man in Montreal's history to be killed by an automobile and seeing the shock of his widow, the terror of his small child. The extraction abandoned Dolores to be just as she had been before, unprepared to cope with subsequent traumas, which her father would therefore continue to extract.

Finally, after we had passed several minutes in the study of each other, Harvey Parrish began to smile.

Once recalled to the Vault, the study of memory became a pastime for me. In the quiet solitude of my dormitory or during conversations with Ettie or Harvey, I found myself captivated by the way memory enriched over time and its capacity for maintaining a number of different contexts at once. A single event, I realized, was like a spool of thread that might be sewn into a dozen separate tapestries. At times that thread would be a scene's primary focus, at others simply a decorative background. Memory could weave thousands of those threads together, and in what became my most intriguing discovery, memory often employed the senses to accomplish it. Textures, sounds, smells could all be time machines, sending a person back through life to discover moments that complemented or matched the present. The phenomenon not only captivated my scientific interest, but also restored a measure of my freedom, transporting me outside the facility. When in the courtyard the wind moved my hair, I might find that it was suddenly 1919 again, and instead of the enclosed space, I was on rue Sainte-Catherine, my hair being moved just as gently by an equally pleasant breeze.

A month after my recall, I spent three days in the sitting room of the Vault watching lawyers and executors and Sources flow in and out. There had never been such an influx of real people underground, to my knowledge, yet something about their hustle and bustle felt familiar. The way both men and women rushed in and out of the visiting area, alternating between impatient attempts at composure and agitated but intentionally hushed bickering. I had some idea what had prompted this rash of real people, but the sound of their overlapping conversations and the muted warmth of the fireplace sent my mind back through time, to a tragic day in March 1909. As in the sitting room, there was still a fireplace at my back, only now it was in Windsor Station and I was waiting for Camille to return to the ladies' waiting room. In a moment she would collect me and we would leave the room to meet the Professor's train. Minutes later, it would be destroyed.

It was St. Patrick's Day. I *know* that but can't be sure it counts as remembering, since the newsreels and papers immediately named the accident for the holiday. We attended no parades, had no plans to witness anything spectacular that day. We only meant to welcome home the Professor—returning from another speaking engagement for which I was the thesis—before the train collided with the station and changed everything.

I can't recall precisely why we left the ladies' room; that's one of the many intermediary details my memory has discarded. In this memory, it's been deemed insignificant, but I suspect that one day, if another tapestry is in need of embroidery, I may remember. Instead of only briefly seeing Camille cross beneath the archway, impatient and excited for the Professor's train to arrive, perhaps I will recall why she asked me to go outside. She may have needed a moment of fresh air and I was willing, both of us hoping a walk would pass the time.

There was a busy crowd outside Windsor Station, and this crowd froze in place after the train crashed into its southern wall, exposing the overnight from Boston. Professor Toutant was on board, and we had no hope of finding him quickly. Deafened by the ungodly sound, we had no hope at all.

There was something misleading about the way the wall busted without entirely breaking. A shattered quiet descended on the station, tuned to the nerves of passersby who were now standing or crouching stunned; then everything began to move again. Voices returned, both agitated and strangely calm. All things considered, the damage to the outside of the station was slight. The damage to the interior of the station was another story altogether. The waiting room was destroyed, run through and collapsing. The concourse, once bright and wide and laced overhead with shimmering beams and precisely wound clocks, was a battlefield—at least that's the way people were describing it. And that's what I remember most: people either rushing around describing graphic images for those of us who couldn't see or else remaining immobile, as though the whole world had shaken and might begin again.

Something in their voices—in their easy paranoia and their willingness to wholeheartedly accept that the end had come—made the moment companion with the present-day scene inside the Vault, despite that, at first, all they seemed to have in common was that they fell on a Wednesday. One was, after all, an apparently harmless event involving people collecting their possessions; it was as benign as any day inside the more traditional banks from which the Vault borrowed its professional language. The other event was of course more devastating, even after we discovered the Professor had escaped unscatched. It was the last of three crashes I'd personally witnessed in my life, each confirming the same lesson: that real life was fragile, and this fragility was born of chaos.

There was one more thing the St. Patrick's Day accident had in common with the mass repossession taking place in the Vault: the murmuring of the women in the crowd, standing farther back, their mouths moving. The Vault's sitting room was separated from the hall by the same wide, dramatic archway I'd seen in Windsor Station, and just on the other side, the women congregated in pairs or trios. The gathering ladies exchanged conversation fragments in whispers too enthusiastic to be low, with eyes cut to track the husbands and fathers collecting their Mems. It had been a week and a half since a teenage Walter Mem descended upon me, and today in the sitting room or in dormitories farther down the hall, Mems were being prepared for departure.

"It's absolutely unacceptable. Unacceptable," said a woman whose hat was embellished with waves of teal velvet. She and the two gathered around her were dressed in nearly identical fur-trimmed jackets that grazed their calves, and I wondered if they'd come together. But for their animated expressions, they almost reminded me of the Dowager Keepsakes.

"Had we known, we never would have left ours," her companion agreed.

"But how would you know?"

"Exactly."

"How would you know." Now they nodded together, absolved of responsibility.

"My Charles only wants to believe the best about Professor Toutant."

"Of course, we all do!"

"But if the clinic can just reprint the ones with bad behavior at their discretion, who's to say it couldn't be ours?"

"And if Professor Toutant can reprint over my Mems, shouldn't he at least have the decency to inform me?"

"Well, you'd like to think so."

"He couldn't very well let some stranger use up *my* Mem, could he? Why then I'd be forced to extract a new one altogether every time I want to rid myself of a memory."

"Oh dear!"

"Well, wouldn't I?"

"I won't have it, girls! I tell you I will *not* end up like one of his crackered-jacks."

I covered my mouth with a shaking hand. How a slur for fractured Sources could be spoken inside the Vault like that, where fractured Sources or their loved ones might hear, was indecent.

"You know, ever since they started hiring nurses, I've been more than a little concerned about just how many people have access," one said as though in direct response to the previous subject. If I hadn't known better, I might have thought the three were neither listening to one another nor keeping track of their conversation's point. "They say this is a discipline of science."

"It used to be, anyway," another interjected.

"But if you ask me, girls will be girls," the woman concluded, as though the irony were lost on her.

"And if that weren't bad enough, what are we to make of his dragging a Source to court? Where will *that* end?"

"You know which Source it is, don't you?" The teal velvet leader quieted them with the promise of an answer. "Dolores. Shepherd."

"*The* Dolores?"

"Have you met her or the Mem?"

"I haven't, personally. Frankly, I find those galas an awful bore."

"Oh, so do I."

"Have you met them?"

"No, no, I haven't."

"But that's worse, isn't it? Dolores Shepherd made him what he is. If he'll quarrel with her, why, none of us are safe."

Which was why, I told myself, the three women were retrieving their Mems today, this instant! Professor Toutant wouldn't be taking ownership of their personal memories, thank you very much.

"And all because they say the Mems were quarreling."

"Talk about impossible."

"Who knows what they've gotten up to in this Vault."

I'd turned to face them several moments before they noticed, the room's contained fire no match for the heat rising up through my neck. It was anger that kept me from looking away, even when their leader raised a suspicious eyebrow in my direction and the others fell quiet.

"She can't understand us, can she?" another of them asked finally, cautious enough to drop her voice.

"My stars, that's *her*."

"Is it?" Two of them leaned together, aghast, and tried to hide their whispers behind cupped hands.

"Of course it isn't," the leader answered without disengaging her glower.

"Oh, I'm mortified, she's one of Dolores's."

"One of them," she spat. "Not *the* one." But her disdain was too palpable. Perhaps my recall hadn't received the attention of my life before, but she had to know I was the famous extract. There was no other explanation for her contempt. "After all"—she took a step in my direction—"it'd be worse than pitiful, wouldn't it, to go from celebrity to a cell?"

I couldn't reply. The woman stood there, staring at me as though her question had been a challenge, and I could say nothing. If she'd meant to humiliate me, to pretend not to know me while exacting a ruthlessly pointed attack, she'd succeeded. I'd done nothing but exist and she hated me for it.

"Anyway. It isn't polite to stare," she told me. "No matter what you are."

Her companions agreed and the trio turned together, setting out down a hall to escape my presence. I gave them a head start so we wouldn't meet again, but try as I might I couldn't quiet my distress. Just like that day outside the train station, my world had been shaken and I'd been wholly unprepared. Sifting through the rubble for survivors had been priority, questions and explanations at first being few. Today, I could not wait for answers. It was me trapped beneath the rubble now, and of all the Sources and saviors taking charge throughout the Vault, none was here to rescue me.

I scanned the many faces in the halls, knowing one had to be a Banker, and finally found Harvey. He was signing a file on the nurses' station where I'd reported the Dolores's expiration. Behind him stood an official-looking gentleman I took to be a lawyer, a couple, and the Mem of a child. At first I thought it might be an extraction from the husband's childhood, but both he and the wife shied away from the Mem as though aware of what it housed. There were too many possibilities to guess, but perhaps they had a son. Then the memory had been extracted either in an attempt at safekeeping, if the son was ill, or for destruction, if the son was not. Deprived of the cinema since returning to the Vault, I would have happily entertained myself exhausting dramatic scenarios for the family. But not today.

When I rushed to his side, resting both my fists next to the file on the counter, Harvey only glanced up but then looked again, this time scrutinizing my forehead while he touched it gently enough not to upset the bruise. When his hand was gone, I could still feel its warmth on my hair and skin.

"I'm a little busy now, Elsie," he said.

The expression about weakening knees turned out to be rather literal, and I dropped my weight to one side so that the desk could support it.

"Are you all right?"

"Oh, yes," I said, my recent upset almost mediated by his deliberately gentle touch, the way he lingered, and the way he'd used my chosen name. "I mean, no." I shook my head, freeing my lips of the smile he'd drawn out of me. "I'm not all right at all."

"You'll have to do better than that."

The nurse behind the desk handed him a new set of files and rattled off a list of appointments, he nodding and drawing the notepad from his pocket. Before I could make my case, he motioned for me to follow him.

"I've only got a moment."

He led me into an empty dormitory. When he closed the door behind us, I sat on one of the stripped beds, but he didn't join me.

"Where are they all going?" I asked, running my hand over the naked mattress.

"To their homes or another private facility."

"Are you worried?"

"There is no shortage of Sources on this island, so that part of the project will no doubt continue as before. This just means we'll have fewer Mems in our care to study."

"You didn't answer my question."

"Is this what upset you, Elsie? The Mems being re-possessed?"

"No."

"Then I don't need to."

I tried not to be offended, taking a moment to glance above the beds. There were no stained-glass windows in this dormitory, only the overhead light. No armoires either. Before I could ask, Harvey cleared his throat impatiently.

"They think I'm lying, for one thing—that Walter's Mem and I quarreled and he didn't attack me at all."

"This isn't about you," he said, shaking his head. "They think the Professor is lying. He's the one giving testimony to legal counsel. And they don't anyway; they're only upset at what it could mean." He'd corrected me as though unsurprised that I knew, but now he looked at me curiously.

"I overheard some women talking, that's all. Sources in the hall just now. And worse, they were accusing the Professor of taking ownership of people's Mems and reprinting them at his discretion."

Harvey nodded, as though it could possibly be true.

"Why would he do that?"

"He hasn't. Not yet. But if a court finds it in the general interest and if the board agrees, violent Mems already housed in the Vault, Mems like the Walter who assaulted you, will become property of the clinic and subject to immediate reprinting."

Immediate reprinting.

"But what will they be reprinted with?"

"Whatever Dolores can't live with this time, I suppose."

When I began to smile again, it was different. Along with an unfamiliar rush of blood, it came from somewhere so much deeper than my skin, from a place I'd never known of and that I hadn't felt before.

Reprinting was an expiration sentence. But I needn't be the one reprinted.

"You proposed this," I said. "For me."

"Selective repossession and reprinting would be a universal mandate," he began.

"But you said Dolores. Whatever *Dolores* can't live with." When he didn't respond, I stood and approached him, watching him straighten as I came near. "Of course the mandate will apply to all of the Vault; it would have to. But you had me in mind, didn't you?"

He tried to scoff, or else something caught in his throat.

"Harvey."

"Elsie," he said back, then stumbled on his words. "There are still any number of hurdles to consider."

"Of course." I came closer.

"It's an option we'd be able to suggest, that Dolores reprint another available Mem. But we couldn't go so far as to compel her. Not under this mandate. Not as it's written now."

"I understand. Cross my heart."

"All right."

"I only want you to admit you're the one responsible, that it was you who proposed it."

In films, the leading man would have taken my face in his hands, my eyelashes batting incessantly. By the movement of his lips and the dramatic motion of his head, I could guess what the title card would read: affection spelled out in black and white. But this was no film. In the month since my recall, Harvey Parrish had proven incapable of dramatic pantomiming—but not devoid of love. He was a scientist and his affection had been shown in the solving of a complicated dilemma, imperfect as the solution might be. He would not rest until it succeeded.

"It doesn't matter who's responsible," he said, lacing his fingers behind his back. "As long as it's approved."

"It matters to me."

When he lifted his chin, I lifted mine as though some invisible string connected the two, my lips parting again and encouraging him to speak when he opened his slightly.

"And the stained glass and lights in my dormitory? And the armoire? What other Mem would need them?" I asked, my voice growing quieter so that neither of us could step away. I was both warm and cold, my skin glowing and goose-pimpled. "Did the Professor commission those?"

Before he could decide whether to lie, I continued.

"Because he wouldn't have. My Professor doesn't want me comfortable here; he wants me released. It had to be you then. Before you'd ever met me."

My new smile widened; all his resistance was finally expired.

"You found me out, Elsie," he said, responding in a voice low enough to match mine, though his quiet seemed born of caution. "I felt like I knew you, long before you came."

My breath quickened but I said nothing.

"I've known your face all my life. First from my father's pictures, in your file that he kept in his office at home. The way your skin deepens somehow while the others go pale. The way he said immediately that you were something more. I knew your voice, from the recordings he listened to constantly. Even while you were living with the Professor for the first free year and then while you lived alone, my father was always worrying over you."

"And did you? Worry over me?"

"No. Never."

I held my own cheek in the cup of my hand, closing my eyes to listen to the smile changing his voice.

"I mooned. I watched the movie reels from the social events, from a brunch with your mah-jongg club and from the night you went to the Mount Royal Hotel debut. It was difficult to look away. You were always stunning."

I'd never been a Dolores to him, never just another extraction of my Source, whose wedding he'd attended (though he could not recall the dress she'd worn). The night I'd felt most glamorous, Harvey Parrish had seen *me*.

"How old were you by then?" I asked, my eyes still closed, my smile still cradled in the palm of my hand.

"Twenty-two." His voice was amused. "I'd just arrived at the Vault. Finally. And you weren't here. Of course you weren't. And I was glad."

I opened my eyes. That part I didn't understand—why would he be glad over my absence? I let it pass easily; even real people mustn't understand everything.

"I'm here now," I told him.

And his chest swelled. "Yes. You are."

Surely he would reach for me now. I knew by the way his brow fell, as though realizing he always could have.

"But now that you're here..."

The light in his eyes whispered a million lovely things that he had yet to say—things that he would, in time. The promise made the prospect of life under lock and key bearable.

"Seeing you inside these walls, I understand. It's because you must be here that I remember what you are."

My shoulders crept up slowly—too slowly to protect myself from the words I'd felt more than heard.

What you are.

The part of me I hadn't known before meeting Harvey was woefully unguarded, but I'd realized it too late. Because immediately I knew what he meant. I'd heard those words before, in my mother's voice, though she'd written them down.

I'd told no one that she'd ever spoken to me, the hurt having been too devastating to share. My first Banker gave me the family address, though he didn't think the correspondence wise. He'd seen the way Dolores's father ignored me the day we watched Laurence Lesh glide and warned that my mother might do the same. But I knew better.

It is indeed remarkable that you recall Dolores's memories, she'd written after receiving my letter in 1909. In it I'd recounted my earliest and favorite memories of us in sometimes painstaking detail. The portrait she and I had taken the year of my debut and the time it had taken her to perfect my hair. She and I at a piano and voice recital, performing together for the first of many times. The color and the fabric of her favorite dressing gown. The way it felt when it brushed against my face, and the way that I still missed it.

I told her how I lived on my own now, in an apartment by myself where there was always space to visit.

I want to be grateful to have received your letter, she wrote. *But I am not.*

You are as remarkable as Dr. Parrish told us, years ago, and I'll confess that I very nearly forgot what you are. Because I am at once proud of you and everything you have accomplished and am also disturbed by the way you speak of me and of us.

I tried reading the letter aloud so that I wouldn't hear her voice in my head, so that perhaps I would stop imagining her in the dress she'd worn for brunch the day I was extracted.

My daughter, you see, is in the next room as I write this. My Dolores, of which I have but one. If I say that you belong to me, what does that say of her? If I say that you are full of life and intellect, is she not? And so you'll understand why I can't write again and why I'd ask that you don't either.

I am mother of one daughter.

You are not Dolores, and I cannot love a Mem.

In the stripped and sterile dormitory, I might have stumbled back if my legs would allow it. Instead I found myself returned from the past, standing before Harvey, as close as he'd drawn me, and swaying between wishing I'd kept my distance and refusing to take the blame again.

"Is this another of your experiments, Mr. Parrish?" I asked at last. "Testing whether something like me can break? My heart is not imaginary, Doctor. And you are not kind."

His dark, thick eyebrows ribboned handsomely but he remained silent.

"You've said it now. The least you could do is look away."

We were where we'd always been: caged inside the Vault. His hair fell, a section at his temple dangling out of place for the first time. He didn't sweep a hand over it and I didn't reach up to put him back together. He only turned away, leaving me alone in a room that wasn't mine.

I stayed there longer than I meant to, losing track of time while the day began to fade. Finally Ettie found me during her evening rounds, and I told her what he'd done.

"I am a memory," I said at last, and for the first time I believed it. "Now I'll live like one."

The Professor and Camille seemed intentionally mis-matched in every physical way, and it only made the couple more romantic. Where her hair was long, he had none. He had such an exceedingly thin frame that whenever he was in front of Camille, she was only partially hidden, her ample curves visible on either side of his. He was a tall man—almost comically so when he stood side by side with his wife—and he had to bend forever for his lips to reach her forehead. It was a sight I'd been missing ever since my recall.

I could pick them out of any crowd, from any distance, and when I knew they were coming, I used to watch from the balcony of my flat. Of course there were no balconies in the Vault. No windows either. And even if I could have watched for them, I'd have seen only Camille. Though she came to visit a second time, I still hadn't seen her husband.

It was my own fault, I told myself to stave off self-pity. I couldn't have brought the portrait they'd given me as a housewarming gift, but I could have remembered the picture locket I'd received the night of Mount Royal's debut. Or, months before my recall arrived, I could have done as the Professor asked and perhaps never have been forced to leave my flat at all.

He and Camille had come to dinner, an occurrence that was too common to be immediately suspicious. But that night in the late spring of 1925, as soon as his wife had volunteered to clear our dinner plates and disappeared into my kitchen before I could protest, his demeanor changed.

"Ma petite," he began. And it wasn't that he dropped his voice—there were many things he shared with me to spare Camille the discomfort—but that he hesitated after.

"Something's the matter," I noted.

And instead of continuing, he smiled at me, a half dozen folds growing around his twinkling eyes.

"You are perceptive, Dolores. As ever."

"Thank you," I answered, so that he would quickly continue.

"If ever things should change," he said, "I'd like you to promise me something."

He stood then, peeking into the next room where Camille could be heard rinsing dishes and asking whether we'd like coffee. Satisfied that his wife was otherwise engaged, he took the seat on the other side of me and laid his hand over mine.

"I've given it a lot of thought, ma petite, so you must trust me."

"I always have before, but you're making me nervous."

"I don't mean to. I just want you to promise me that if ever Dolores should try to take you back, if ever you're recalled to the Vault, you must elect to have a Mem extracted."

The air between us was still.

"A Mem of your own."

"No."

"At least consider it."

"My answer would stay the same."

"Dolores, listen—"

"After everything I've seen in your office? You knew I wouldn't agree to that. How could I?"

I wish I hadn't spoken so harshly when I could see the faint grief in his eyes. It was distant, dread for a heartache he'd yet to suffer, but it was there.

"I would not ask except in the most extreme circumstance."

"And even then, I would never do it."

At the time, recall *was* the most extreme circumstance I could imagine. I knew nothing of reprinting then, and anyway, the worst scenario a Mem could face was not inside the Vault, but at home, sequestered with the Source and punished for existing. The Professor was not the only one who'd helped a Mem expire, though he might've been the only one to do so without violence. Still, I was not the sort of Mem destroyed by a Source. I wasn't born of a humiliating memory or a trauma personally endured; what was once my family had no reason to harbor disgust or hold my presence against me. It'd been years since they acknowledged my existence at all.

"It wouldn't be a memory of consequence," the Professor insisted.

"Which memories aren't?"

"Not a memory then, ma petite. A moment. Only long enough to demonstrate that you can."

"But we don't even know that I can, if I'm allowed." I tried to stop but couldn't. I sounded the way Dolores's mother told her never to be. Contrarian. My memory of that warning had stayed me writing her back once I'd received her letter. Yet there I was, arguing with the Professor because I didn't know yet what was at stake.

"You can." His fingers tightened around mine. "I'm sure of it. And as far as allowances, no one needs to know until we've done it."

"And what would it prove?" I asked. "You wouldn't ask unless you thought it proved something, and we needed that proof." He didn't answer then, and that should have been answer enough. "Would it prove that I'm not a Mem after all? That I am my own?"

"Yes!"

"I am proving that now, right this moment, by saying no. Yes, I *belong* to someone, to Dolores, technically, but it doesn't matter. It never has."

"It has always mattered, petite." Where I had spoken emphatically, he was suddenly calm. Or quiet, at least. "It's why you cannot come and go as you please, why you've never lived anywhere but Montreal—"

"I've never wanted to."

"Things change, Dolores. People, too. It's part of being alive." He waited a long while, watched me almost without blinking. "Please."

"I'm sorry." And he deflated. "I don't believe in it. I know it's your life's work, Professor, but I don't agree with the practice of extraction. That's the truth. What kind of people are we if we can't traverse the landscape of our own memories? What kind of people do they become who refuse?"

"It's one procedure."

"So was hers."

He closed his eyes, and I waited until the sound of Camille singing put him at ease.

"And I know the length would be different and you don't think there'd be so great a risk, but I don't care. I'd lose something either way."

Looking back, he may not have been listening anymore. He knew much more than I did by then.

"Maybe she regained her composure and the extraction seemed worthwhile, but maybe Dolores never had another chance to experience what I did, staring at that broken widow and man. Maybe instead of making her stronger, it weakened her. Maybe she couldn't cope with anything that happened after," I said, because I didn't yet know that I'd been the catalyst for her second extraction.

He might've told me then what Dolores had become, but he didn't. Instead he accepted my refusal with what in hindsight could only be a father's magnanimous humility.

The bittersweet confliction of pride in the child's ability to reason for herself and pain in the knowledge that she will fail. That I would never be a real girl, and he was helpless to change that.

"I don't want to be like Walter," I said, foolish enough to think his silence empty. I at least had the good sense to speak the next part gently. "I don't want to be like any of them."

He nodded then, his eyes on our hands, the sound of Camille's voice drifting ahead of her before she jovially reentered the dining room and, with a curtsy, presented us with the evening's coffee.

He didn't ask me again. Even when I called the house while I held the telegram in my trembling hands. Camille's weepy voice met my ear and it was she who needed consoling, so I pulled myself together. I insisted that if the Professor knew about the recall and there really had been no mistake, I could manage to the Vault on my own.

Harvey and I came to an agreement without speaking. We'd somehow arranged at what time he would be in the sitting room and at what time I could visit it without fear of running into him. We'd settled that I would stay largely in my dormitory, stepping out of view of the hall when I heard the distant tenor of a man's voice that might turn out to be his, and nearly tiptoeing to Ettie's station when she was too busy to steal me aboveground for a walk in the courtyard.

Today she walked into my room with the boxy radio under one arm and two cafeteria plates in hand.

"I brought you something special," she said when I didn't get out of bed to greet her.

"There's nothing special about the radio except that it's in my room."

"No, doll, it's better."

She bent at the knees, both hands still full, and opened her arm to let the radio fall on the neighboring bed.

"It's heartbreak food. Real girls eat dessert first thing in the morning when someone's made us sore." She sat down beside me. "I do, anyway."

Rising up onto an elbow, I accepted the plate and took stock of its contents. When I had, I couldn't stop myself from crying and Ettie hurried to close my door.

"It isn't Harvey," I said, vacillating between a light laugh and heavier tears. "It's everything now. It's this." I looked down at the layered gelatin and accoutrement. "Neapolitan and custard on a milk glass plate."

It seemed like foolishness to cry now, over a cake plate, when I hadn't cried before. Not when my father ignored me in 1907 or when Harvey's father informed me that I wouldn't see Dolores or her father again, and not when I read my mother's letter. No one would have guessed its contents, I hid my response so well. I'd kept the envelope on my writing desk near the door so that when company came and someone asked—my nosy super on her way out or a short-lived friend I'd see only a few times more—I could say who it was from.

"Real people assume it must be lovely," I explained between tiny bites. "That she must have written me lovely things."

"But it's not true of every mother and child, Mem or not. Scores of families are hideous, Elsie, they are."

"But they aren't. Dolores's parents aren't hideous. They're just hers." I laughed then while I wiped my eyes, dessert spoon in hand. "Why is memory this way? Why isn't it content to hurt you once? Why must it remind you of all the times you've been hurt before?"

"Oh, Elsie, dear." My friend laid her head against mine for a moment, both our hands too busy still feeding ourselves to hug the other. "It's all that Banker's fault."

Finally I set my plate aside.

"If you had any sense, you'd leave me alone," I said.

"I know." She offered me her last bite when it was already on her spoon and I accepted. "I had thought what it'd do to me if the reprint erased you."

"Had you?"

She nodded, taking both our plates and setting them on the other bed near the still silent radio.

"It would've, you know. Erased me. If not for Harvey's mandate."

She nodded again. Because, of course, she knew. In the eight weeks since I returned and since her tenure began, there had been at least a handful of reprints performed on Mems who lived in the Vault. Ettie had assisted with more than one removal since the night we'd met, escorting a technician to the part of the clinic where expired Mems went and then coming back to those of us who were still alive.

"I think that it'd be torture, seeing you here and knowing you didn't remember me."

"My stupid, stupid heart," I said, flicking a tear away.

"What's it done?"

"Realized how Harvey must have felt that very same way."

"Intent to love them all anyway, aren't you?" Ettie sighed, falling back against my headboard and cutting her eyes to catch mine. "If you aren't a real girl, Elsie, then neither am I."

It was Ettie who told me the Professor was coming later that same day. I knew that it mattered, his coming now, and that it meant that soon my life would change.

He towered in the doorframe when he arrived, looking nothing like the Walter Mem; instead of terror, the sight of him filled me with concern. I could see that he was overwhelmed and it permitted me to admit that I was, too. It could have been years since we'd seen each other last, and the thought that I'd lost track of time in the Vault—that these eight weeks had taken a greater toll than any spent aboveground—frightened me.

"Ma petite," he said.

At the sound of his voice, I exploded off the bed, nearly falling in the race to his arms. And the first thing I wanted to tell him was how the world had broken my heart. It had happened one person at a time, I wanted to say, but Harvey Parrish had dealt the crippling blow.

Still, I didn't. A lifetime had passed since the night at my dining table. Now I could hold my tongue. Now I knew I wasn't the headstrong girl my Professor had raised me to be. No matter what Ettie said, I wasn't a girl at all.

"I'm a Mem," I said into the tweed of his vest, as though into the starchy veil of a confessional.

He took my face in his large hands, his palms warming my cheeks and chin, his long fingers curving over my temples.

"T'es ma petite," he answered, as if that were something else entirely.

He led me up the stairwell and past reception in the same outfit I'd worn the day I surrendered myself. They'd been my favorite heels for traipsing the city streets—the lace-up oxford pumps in burgundy leather—and I always felt smart matching them with the cap-sleeved lace dress with the burgundy sash that sat low on the hips. I smiled when I was back in my own clothing, relieved that I'd dressed so well for recall now that I was going to meet the man who'd wanted to marry me. The man who'd married Dolores.

"It hasn't gone well, my dear," the Professor confided when we were still in my dormitory. "I'd hoped they might see reason before it got this far. And I suppose they thought the same of me."

"I've seen the Mems being repossessed," I said, so he needn't relive the entire ordeal in explaining it to me.

"The project is suffering a bit of backlash because of my taking Dolores to court, I'll admit it. I was prepared to accept that."

I tipped my head to catch his falling gaze and smiled encouragingly.

"The board was not. They won't allow for an appeal if it comes to that, and it will. I'm certain they'd refuse to compel any Source to spare their Mem—especially Dolores Shepherd. They won't allow for any more fighting at all."

The Professor tossed his own head to the side as though casting off regard. "Oh, but how many of them care for anything but the welfare of the stockholders, and how many of *them* worry about anything but a return on their investments?!"

He laughed disgustedly, but only for a moment. Then he looked me in the eyes. "It's a mess, Dolores. All of it." He held my face between his great hands again and I covered them with my own. "I thought they'd all see reason."

"No one cares for me the way you do."

"I can't accept that," he said. "We've just been appealing to the wrong men."

"So now we appeal to Mr. Shepherd?"

He didn't have to nod to confirm what I had thought when he'd phoned to tell me about the meeting: we were going to beg for salvation from the only person who had the power over Dolores to grant it.

The quiet that fell between us persisted. Allowing only the sharp echo of our steps, it accompanied us beyond the reception desk and down the many halls, past laboratories where Mems were extracted and one more where the corpses of the expired were taken for dismemberment—the only room in which we were truly safe from the threat of reprinting. It was the room into which I, like all the others, would someday be carried. Where my organs would be harvested for study or donation. Because loved or not, expiration was inevitable. By nature or by the hand of the one who'd refused to carry it anymore, a Mem had no other destiny. It was a thought upon which I'd never settled before returning to the Vault. It was a fate I might never have believed if Harvey hadn't reduced me to it.

We crossed the courtyard separating the clinic from the Professor's office. There, Lyman Shepherd waited. He stood when the Professor held the door open for me.

"Dolores, this is Mr. Shepherd."

"Lyman," the man said quickly. "Ly." And then he smiled and I knew that must be what the real Dolores called him. It was the smile he might have offered if I'd made it from the coach to the restaurant without that fatal accident interrupting. Where the Professor stood now, my father might have been, and the inside of this office would never have existed for me. I stopped myself there, unsure whether I'd ever had this train of thought before and whether it was as harmless as it felt at first. Regardless, Lyman was a stranger to me, with his dapper auburn hair parted far on the right and swept back in a fashion that was certain to hold—but he knew me.

It was a funny way to clean up a mess, I thought, placing a younger version of a man's wife before him, but the public proceedings could not go on. Not if the Professor hoped to salvage his career and maintain ownership of the facility and the study he'd built. It was a threat I knew wouldn't have frightened him until someone explained that he'd lose more than that. Camille must have, or Harvey. Someone who knew that the life he'd given me was only possible because of what he'd accomplished, because of the respect attached to his name and the generosity of first Dolores's father and then the Shepherds. So that someone else might also have offered him one more strategy. And here we were, the Professor and his secret adviser hoping that Lyman Shepherd would recognize my uniqueness and convince Dolores not to reprint me. I could see from the Professor's knitted brow and the way his hand crept around mine that he had considered nothing beyond that—certainly not the poorly contained excitement that flickered through Mr. Shepherd's smile.

"Your hair was longer."

My fingers resisted the urge to reach for the blunt ends of my modern bob. Instead, I nodded curtly.

"I like it," he said quickly, his smile spreading slowly. "I've always preferred shorter hair on you." I told myself it was only natural that someone who knew Dolores—the real and original—would speak to me as though I were her. "It frames your face well."

"Mr. Shepherd, we've never met," I couldn't help but point out. "How could you have any preference about me at all?"

He continued to smile as though I'd spoken sweetly, and since I hadn't raised my voice or stormed out, perhaps only the Professor could see my agitation.

"Where is she?" I asked.

"Dolores? At home. She doesn't like to come beyond the West Island."

"I'd like to meet her first."

"Nothing's been decided, *petite*," the Professor whispered.

"I could take you."

When the Professor shot Lyman a disapproving glare, the younger man cleared his throat.

"If you'd like to meet her, I could escort you to our home. If that's all right with Professor Toutant."

"Well, it's you and Dolores who own me, isn't it? I'm sure you can take me wherever you please."

My sterile honesty did not sit well with the Professor, and he spoke almost before I'd finished. "Mr. Shepherd, will you excuse us for a moment?"

His eyes shifting once between the Professor and I, Lyman dipped his head and let himself out. The Professor kept his stance for a moment. Like a sentinel on guard, he lifted his chin slightly, his arms at his side, his hands closing into fists and then releasing.

"I apologize," I said, still watching his hands until he looked at me. "Beneath this floor it was easy to forget how much you cared, but I shouldn't have. You've been fighting in a way I'm not allowed and it means the world to me."

Now his jaw clenched as well, so that the only softness I could see was in the tears shivering on his lower eyelids before slipping down his face.

"I'm not giving up," he managed, as though his voice fought to escape. "They refused mediation at first, and now he's agreed to meet you. That's a start. It's a good sign, Dolores. So you must promise me that you won't give up either."

"If I'm a Mem, it isn't giving up."

I didn't say that real people may do as they like with their memories or that perhaps my Professor was most afraid because of what he himself had done. But his shoulders buckled forward as though I had or as though I hadn't needed to. When he caught himself on the chairback before him, I leaped to his side for the second time in our life together. My embrace forced him to correct his posture enough to wrap an arm around me, his forehead resting against mine.

"I cannot lose another child."

It was the loveliest thing ever said to or about me and it broke my heart in an entirely new way. I'd become as vain as any of the other Mems; despite what I knew about him, I'd forgotten that not every real person had chosen the path of relief. Like me, the Professor had kept his mind intact. His memories remained—even the ones that tormented him, the ones that kept him from ever speaking freely with his wife. These same ones now terrified him. It was as if I could somehow read his mind; I could feel his anxiety at the thought that Lyman Shepherd might do to me what the Professor had done to Camille No. 1, but reason—or optimism—assured me that my Source's husband had no such provocation.

"You can't lose me," I whispered. "I'll always be your girl. Even if you're the only one to see me that way."

As much as I hoped breaking with the fantasy of humanness would simplify my life, I couldn't help the way they stayed on my mind, these parents who had chosen me, the Professor and Camille, and Ettie, my last and closest friend.

And Harvey.

"Let me go with Lyman. You saw the way he looked at me. If he likes me, perhaps they'll accept another Mem to be reprinted in my place."

"The board wants all fighting to end," he said.

"I know."

"There's no one to take your place." I nodded, though I already understood. He was recalling the facts for his own benefit, so that he could do what needed to be done. "No other Dolores Mem exists and we've been awarded no right to the others."

I took his hands in mine. "Lyman is our only chance."

He was composed now, but in his eyes I could see him calculating the risk. As though they could run away with me, somehow reprint me on their own. Or as though they might now decide to keep me for themselves.

"Please, Professor," I said, before confessing, "I want to go. I want to see Dolores again no matter what happens."

He stood tall, tugging with both hands at the rim of my hat before patting the top. He seemed to know this already, which was odd, because I'd only realized it now. Regardless the outcome, I wanted to meet my Source.

A pale blue sky inspired a symphony of incessant bird calls despite the chill. Standing out in the open—not simply in the more spacious cage of the clinic's terrace—I looked to both corners of the sky in search of clouds. The weather shifted quickly this time of year, and in the distance, somewhere else on the island, I saw evidence of a light rain. Outside the Vault, Montreal was just as lovely and fickle as I'd left it.

The Professor kept his hand curled around the open window after closing me into the passenger's side of the Shepherd automobile.

"I'll send a car this evening?" He tried to smile.

"That'll be fine, Professor." Lyman leaned toward the opening and I pulled myself back into my seat.

The Professor took my chin in his hand for a moment and then stepped away, giving the vehicle space to maneuver. After that, Lyman left me alone to enjoy the cityscape until we were out of Centre-Ville, the cluster of tall, ornate buildings replaced first by a view of Mont Royal and then a much flatter, calmer terrain. Though he repeatedly glanced at me while still appearing attentive to the road, I said nothing. Whatever kept him mystified was none of my concern, I'd decided. Whatever real people deigned or did not bother to tell me was their prerogative, and I should learn to feel nothing on the matter.

Finally, he broke with pretense and turned a bit in his seat so that he could see me more readily while he drove.

"Forgive me, I just can't seem to reconcile this."

"Oh?" I shouted over the car engine, as if to cover my own irreconcilable thoughts. It was impossible to relegate Harvey's image to the back of my mind, and at the moment it seemed undeniably due to Lyman's presence. But why? The two men didn't resemble each other in any way. Lyman was bred for society life. To be honest, by the way he stood when I first laid eyes on him, Lyman Shepherd reminded me of the champion stallion introduced to us when the Professor, Camille, and I visited Blue Bonnets years before. Princely and fortunate, everything about his appearance was expensive, though somehow the exact cost was kept intimidatingly quiet. When I was a part of Dolores, Lyman was exactly the type of man I'd expected to marry. He smiled easily and, most likely, often. He was the type I knew I should find immediately charming and imagined that if he'd been outside the restaurant that day when I'd fallen into hysterics, he'd have known exactly what to say to calm me down. Whether he'd sided with my father or voted against the clinic, his decision would have been altogether reasonable. And he would never have worn a cologne, let alone one as strong as Harvey's. When I was lucky, I still sometimes caught that fragrance on the edge of the Vault's circulated air.

"You're the age you were when we met, but you don't know me. It's terribly odd." He glanced at the road and then returned to me as though helpless to resist. "You don't remember. You're not my wife. But you are. It's impossible."

"I know what you mean," I ventured. "I know of you; I know I was on my way to meet you but never did. Even though, had I not been extracted, I would be part of the Dolores you know so well."

And immediately I felt my face flush with heat at the way my words might be interpreted. The inside of my hands immediately damp, I wrung them together in my lap. If my word choice hadn't similarly struck Lyman, he most certainly inferred the accidental innuendo by my obvious embarrassment. Strange that he would lay his hand over mine then, as though touching me would lessen the discomfort. I kept my palms clasped together so that his curling fingers couldn't reach them. At least when he released me nothing more was said until after we left the main road and passed beneath a wrought-iron archway.

Lush emerald grass tapered at the edges of a gray gravel stream wide enough for a single automobile to travel. Rosebushes sprang up on either side as the stream ran up an impressive incline, at the top of which was a wide, statuesque home the likes of which could not be readily found in the city. There was a flagpole on top and two flags lapped at the air: one American, the second my blue-and-white Fleurdelisé. Their bodies took turns curling and unfurling so that only one was fully visible at a time. As we approached, the flagpole ran down as though into the hill itself, except that the closer we came, the more the home grew beneath it. My eyes traveled from the iron fencing of the widow's walk down two stories, admiring gables on either side. Much care had been taken with the precise placement atop the hill, and the architect had more than succeeded with the building's slow, dramatic reveal.

"I remember the first time you saw it. Such a fond memory."

I kept my eyes on the manor. Along with his fond memory, it must have been what made him smile.

"It wasn't this blue-gray color then," he said, though with the innumerable windows and decorative brackets, the muted color was almost overwhelmed by the white trim. "Your eyes were twice as wide as they are now."

Lyman parked the car and hurried around to let me out before his hold of my arm caught my attention.

"You do still like it, Dolly?"

"It's gorgeous." I praised the house if only to speak over the pet name that surely belonged to his wife. In the moment that followed, all I could feel was his warm hand on the bare skin of my elbow. "What color was it originally?"

He stepped back and turned to face the house as though he, too, were seeing it for the first time.

"Sort of a rose. Or salmon, Dolores once called it. I don't know the difference." I was becoming accustomed to the occasional revelation of a dimple in his right cheek, which I now admired, rather than trying to explain how very different one color was from the other. "Whatever it was, it was the color of my childhood home."

"In New England," I recalled, and he spun around as though I'd performed some impressive feat. Perhaps I should have disabused him of the notion, reminding him that my father told me *something* about each new suitor and that if I tried I could probably still remember them all, if not by name than by minutiae. Of course we'd been taught never to speak of the others, back when I was part of Dolores, and certainly once married never to speak as though there had been many.

"In New England, yes. I was born in a house exactly like this one. But I never wanted to go back once I met you."

"Instead you built a replica," I said through the misleading whimsy of a sigh.

As though on cue, the front door opened and a figure stepped out onto the dark porch, a shadow cast across her face by the columns upholding the second-story balcony. She wore a dark dressing gown, and though she did not speak, she quieted us both. After only two uncertain steps, someone reached out from the entryway to guide Dolores back in, and my heart hiccupped, beginning again.

"The house was designed in what's called Queen Anne style," Lyman said, after clearing his throat, his hands by his sides now. "It was rather popular when I was a boy. I suppose I never fully recovered from it because I felt I had to have a second one here."

I took several steps toward the house, Lyman's voice trailing off behind me. He made no move to follow as I went up the steps and crossed between the columns. Reaching for the front door, I looked over my shoulder to see him still beside the car, his mouth hanging slightly open.

Inside, the foyer was dim. A staircase stood on my left, its polished arm sweeping up to the first of several landings, its steps decorated by a wide runner of plush carpet. An opening gaped to my right and, beyond it, the furniture brooded within great pools of shadow. Hissing whispers rushed upon me in swells and I hesitated, hoping to determine into which room Dolores and her attendant had disappeared.

I recognized the voice in the whispers; it was my own.

In the darkness ahead, French doors stood apart, their distance just enough to remind me of quarreling lovers captured in flickering black and white—too far to embrace but close enough to touch. Like Harvey standing in front of me in a dormitory, forever slipping away into the hall. If I hesitated long enough, the doors, whose curtained glass kept everything but the voices within a secret, might have reconciled and shut themselves tight. I hurried through and found the two women together, the attendant perched on the edge of the white silk sofa and Dolores partially reclined as though she'd flung herself there. Her head leaned against one of the extravagant rises of the wingback, and her legs were outstretched at an angle across it so that her attendant had little room on the three-seater. At my entrance, Dolores snapped her fingers twice before kissing at the air like I was the kitten she'd been beckoning.

It was the sight of the attendant that made my heart sink. She was old enough—at least as far as I could tell—but I immediately knew she could not have been our mother. I'd been certain she would not be here, yet something in me, I realized, had been hoping otherwise.

"Mercy," the old woman whispered, the crow's-feet at the corners of her eyes multiplying as she squinted at me. It was a wonder that a woman of her age could manage with so little light in the house.

When I turned to switch on the floor lamp, the woman stood quickly.

"No, no. You'll upset her."

She approached and recommenced her squinting, sweeping away the hair that framed my face and holding it back on my forehead with her palm. Now she could see me uninterrupted. She was not our mother, so something felt strange about the way she studied me. She was a hired nurse at best—though it would confirm my worst fears about Dolores's state if she needed one—and I couldn't imagine why she should look at me as though through a lifetime of memories.

"You've known her for some time?" I asked.

"Long enough to know she must have once looked like you." She held the awed expression for a moment and then—as though she finally saw me—it flickered out. "You shouldn't be here. Mr. Lyman ought to know better."

I had no chance to answer before my own voice interrupted.

"Emma?"

I swallowed as if doing so might confirm that the question had not come from me.

"Emma!" Dolores sang, sitting up now, her hand outstretched in my direction, her fingers splayed as though she was desperate to reach me; yet she did not stand. "Oh, you're all right!"

As soon as my fingers touched hers, they weaved themselves together. Tears rushed to blur my vision but they didn't fall. Whether I had always dreamed of it or whether it was a new sensation, now I longed to be held in her arms—but when I sat next to her, Dolores curled into mine. I smelled the lavender she was still using to cover the smell of the straightening chemicals in her finger-waved hair, and I marveled at the way it felt like mine. Not just similarly, but precisely. When I ran my hand over the hair that darkness could not dull, the sensation was devastating. At first too familiar to register any feeling at all, it was as though I was touching my own. And then a flood of overstimulation, an untranslatable reckoning of our exactness and our separation. An ache because we were one. A flurry of excitement because we were not.

"Who is Emma, Dolores?" I asked her. "Who am I?"

"Look at you," she answered, drawing back with a smile. "Who else could you be?"

When she cradled my bob, she did not sense what I was. Nothing—not my face or my skin or the sound of my voice—could inform Dolores that I'd once been a piece of her. Neither did our sameness grant me any insight into what she had become.

"You're my baby sister, all grown up and gorgeous." Her teeth sat perfectly, one atop the other, and what little light there was made them glimmer. I found myself close to cringing at the thought that they might break.

I didn't have a little sister. Not at nineteen, at least. I didn't have any siblings at all. It seemed unlikely that any had been born later, but how could I know what happened after I was extracted? Perhaps she'd gained a sister in marrying Lyman, though how could that person possibly resemble me? Or perhaps her parents had an unlikely pregnancy later in life and kept me in the dark because of what I am. Because—no matter how remarkable—as Dolores's Mem, I had no right to know. Because no matter what Dolores had become, she retained sole custody of the life that we had shared.

"If I'm your sister Emma, Dolly, then when was I born?" I asked, venturing to use Lyman's name for her, widening my faltering smile.

And then her eyes jumped and her head with them. A moment after I'd spoken, she gasped, drawing in a sharp and short breath and looking at the empty space just beside me.

"Dolores?" said the attendant.

She jerked out of my arms, then shoved me hard enough that I would've fallen had I not stood from the sofa.

"Dolores!" the old woman spoke again, this time chastising, and I looked from her to the woman-child retreating backward into a corner of the couch. Standing between them, I felt a weakness threatening my knees and a hot pounding in my chest, unsure which one would overwhelm me first. There's a chance that I was angry, that I had been all along. Even when I thought that I was tired of fighting, perhaps I was exhausted by having to. But I wasn't angry at her.

"Where are you from, Dolores?" I asked.

It was the only question I could think to ask, the only one I thought simple enough that Dolores would understand, but I shouldn't have. I knew that for certain as soon as the elderly woman struck me. Before I could turn to face her, the attendant's closed fist thudded against my upper arm again. Then, as we locked eyes, the woman opened her palm and slapped me across the face. My skin sizzled and, scratched by her index finger, a well sprang from my left eye.

"How dare you," she growled, as though incapable of opening her mouth any wider. "How dare you ask her that!" She crowded me so that with every phrase, her spit landed on my skin. "Speaking as though you're one of us—as though she's one of you!"

I hardly opened my mouth to respond before her closed fists pounded my shoulder.

"One of you," she said again, the last word partnered with a blow so that the pronoun was made insult and I understood why she was hitting me.

It was an assault I'd imagined could only come from a Source angry at a memory or else at the piece of themselves that had endured, at the Mem that reminded them. But in her heavy breathing and in the shadow where her face should have been, the aging attendant spent what may have been her last reserves proving she'd been made a kind of surrogate Source. Hidden in the dark with what was now less than half a woman, she must have hated me as much as she hated Dolores. In truth, she hated me more.

"Look at her," she shouted, her blows intensifying. "And look at you! You took her life with you, you wretch."

I both heard and felt a crack before I tasted metal in my mouth.

"You've taken my life, too, you beast!"

And suddenly I was thinking of my Professor. Of Harvey and Camille and Ettie, too, but the Professor first. What he would go through when he found out and how he would blame himself when I was dead. Because I knew from the strength that did not match her stage in life that the woman would not stop. She wasn't Walter's Mem; I had not gotten tangled in a memory. Every blow was meant for me, and outside of the Vault, there was no one to intervene.

At first I was shaking too violently to realize that the beating had stopped. I'd heard Dolores scream with my voice but hadn't noticed when she'd gotten up from the couch. After that came the sound of glass breaking, and when I looked, the attendant was crumpled in front of the French doors, a point of impact where her back had collided with the glass.

Through tears both protective and organic, I saw Dolores standing between our collapsed bodies, her chest heaving from the excitement or from the effort of having flung her attendant off me. As she watched me now, her eyes grew wild and a horrible confusion drained her face of color. When Dolores began to scream again, it almost covered the heavy gallop of Lyman running from the front door. Before he could reach us, I offered my hand to her, and she took it. Still like touching my own flesh, trying to discern the end of my skin and the beginning of hers was as futile as tickling myself.

"Dolores." I clasped her hands, squeezing them in earnest as the screaming settled into moans, but the confused expression persisted.

This was what thirty-eight looked like, on Dolores at least. She didn't look as frazzled as the Mem who'd expired in my dormitory what seemed like ages ago. Of course she didn't. Whatever had upset the real Dolores had been stripped away, reprinted over an already beleaguered shell who'd carried who knew how many unwanted memories beneath. This Dolores was nineteen years older than me, but holding her soft hands in mine, I knew: she was not equipped for this. The damage was done. She could not place me—her father had seen to that. But perhaps she was the remarkable one, because something made her try. I was remarkable because of who she was.

"Dolores, who is Emma?"

"I don't know," she whispered penitently, squeezing my hands. Shifting her weight from one foot to the other, she glanced several times at Lyman, just inside the door, who had been arrested by the sight of the crumpled older woman. Whatever I wanted to know had to be spoken now, in this moment.

"You don't have a sister?"

She shook her head, and I shushed her gently before she could begin to scream again.

"I don't know. I couldn't," and then she drew her lips into her mouth as though this, too, was an apology. "But you look like me."

The brown skin of her forehead creased like a drape of sweet fondant and her grimace renewed each time it seemed on the verge of dissipating.

"I'm me," she said. "Why do you look like me?"

And then I just said it, to save her the way she'd saved me. It came out easily, as though it had always been true.

"I'm Elsie. We used to be friends."

For a moment, it seemed like it wouldn't be enough. Her hands were still a bit slick from being pressed against mine, her forehead still creased. Only slowly the storm in her eyes calmed. Her posture relaxed and she stood evenly on both feet.

"Elsie." The heaviness in her breath relaxed. "You're Elsie then. And I'm Dolores."

"That's right," I agreed, and even in the faint light, hand in hand with my Source, I could see that my skin was darker and now I knew why. "I am Elsie. And you are Dolores."

It seemed each building that went up in the city of Montreal was more splendid than the last and, in 1924, the Rialto was no exception.

Camille and I were unescorted that late December evening when the Park Avenue theater made its formal opening. The busy sidewalk glowed beneath a halo of innumerable neon lights, and all the way up the bustling lobby steps Camille regaled me with the ways in which the theater resembled the Paris Opera that had been its inspiration. She pointed out every gold embellishment, every frescoed cherub, and recalled the first time she'd been to the City of Light and how long it had been since last she'd gone.

"You'll see," she promised, patting the back of my gloved hand, our arms linked at the elbow. "We'll get you off this island if it kills me."

She couldn't know that the following year I'd be even more captive, locked in the Vault underground with only the promise of reprinting to look forward to. She couldn't know it then and neither did I, so instead of mounting a defense of the only city I'd seen outside of newsreels and Dolores's memories, I agreed.

"Nothing compares to Paris, honestly, but—" and then she gasped, beholding the balcony view for the first time. "This certainly suffices for now."

We'd come to see Virginia Valli in a story set in Paris, coincidentally or not. It was that picture, in fact, that inspired Camille's long overdue decision to shorten her hair. Of fashionable women in society, Camille had been the singular hold out. Perhaps it was her ample frame that discouraged her, for fear that cutting her hair would expose her. But that evening changed her mind entirely.

"I've been told I resemble Virginia, you know," she said, eyes widening the way they often did when it was just she and I. When free of men she became just a bit more enthusiastic, even daring. It was a security I understood all the more once I'd befriended Nurse Ettie. "I've a bit more roundness to my face, of course," Camille was saying, still fiddling with her appearance. "But her hair is nearly as thick as mine and I think it looks darling, don't you?"

It was the kind of conversation in which I'd not felt entirely fluent since my extraction. I could recall the way Dolores had once talked incessantly with girlfriends, trading anecdotes and insights on fashion and appearance and society life, but that had been some time ago. For my part, I had Camille and the Professor and the disparate manners in which I conversed with each, and I couldn't help assigning more relevance and interest to the nature of things I spoke of with him. While my friendship with Camille reminded me sometimes of life before the extraction—of the blessing of female companionship and love—it seemed to be those discussions with the Professor that grounded me in the life I was leading now, that kept me from lamenting all the failed friendships since. Those talks—and his occasional revelations, be they bleak or disenchanting—informed my understanding of the world and the people in it. So when Camille caught sight of a mother searching for a pair of seats, her little girl in tow, I knew what made Camille's breath stop, even as she most certainly did not.

We'd chosen balcony seats beneath the decadent stained-glass ceiling. Framed with exquisite moldings in colors so vibrant I couldn't help but smile up at them, the concave space narrowed toward what seemed at first to be a skylight. Had we not just come in from the chilly winter's night, I may have wondered whether it was the sun that shone so brightly behind the glass above my head. Even with something unique to see in every direction, the faux skylight could not be outdone. Not even when I had stained glass of my own, in the Vault, would that theater be called to comparison.

Camille had been sharing my adoration of the design only moments before, but now she'd fallen quiet. When finally I recognized the uncharacteristic silence, I found her watching the mother and child intensely, turned in her seat to keep the pair in view. It seemed she couldn't help herself, even when the couple sitting behind us noticed her staring as well and began giving her silent remonstrations. Finally, the little girl and her mother sat down and Camille returned to me—or else I saw the crest of her eyebrows releasing, her eyes glistening while she bit her lip.

I put my hand on hers and she smiled sheepishly.

"I don't know what's the matter with me," she said, her cheeks and chest flushing. But then her expression became one of sincerity and a wrenching sadness she should not have remembered. "There's something about seeing a mother and her little girl. I just..."

Now she was self-conscious, glancing around before touching the skin above her mouth, either to hide it or to shield the outside world from whatever she meant to say.

"Dolores, I swear, it feels like my heart could break." She dug into her shallow clutch for a handkerchief and lowered her head to discreetly wipe her eyes. "At first it seems so reasonable—I've always wanted children, after all. But then I end up feeling like I'm just a little crazy." A fresh surge of anguish overwhelmed her for a moment. "Oh, I apologize. How can it ache so horribly when I don't even know what I'm missing? I've no excuse for this."

If I said something—the agreeable things I could say without betraying the Professor and destroying Camille, and probably her marriage, too—it would only make her more uncomfortable. She would abuse herself, say she should know better than to be such a dramatic old bird, and then apologize me into silence. So instead I kept quiet, mimicking the aloof behavior of other Mems and hoping she might assume the situation was simply too complex for me to understand. Despite our long history, she always let me. And because I knew more of hers than she remembered, it didn't bother me. I was part of the charade now, no longer an innocent caught between two worlds. Like the Professor and Dolores's parents and countless others, I'd become defender of the illusion. Curator of a false history.

While Camille put away her handkerchief and flicked the last tears from her cheeks, I gave her something like a smile and she offered a nervous titter in return. "Anyway. Forget I said anything. I wish the lights would go down, at least."

For the rest of the night and while we headed back into the winter evening, Virginia Valli's hairdo was all Camille could talk about.

Almost a year later, in October 1925, I discovered that emotional residue was not an experience limited to Sources. Lyman Shepherd was a case study in how those who loved Sources could suffer a variation of the phenomenon all their own.

After putting his wife to bed and collecting some of the broken glass into a dustpan, he'd joined me in his kitchen with his "auto kit," a tin box stocked with emergency first aid materials. Dolores's attendant was fine, he told me, only too proud to face anyone. Lyman's implication was that she'd embarrassed herself with her violent outburst, but I doubted that she cared much about that—it'd been Dolores's response that humiliated her. The fact that anyone would defend a Mem. In any event, Lyman wasn't upset with me. Pensive, yes. Or maybe he was simply waiting to see what my response would be.

"Did my parents ever have more children?" I asked, leaning against the cold porcelain tile of the counter. My hands flat against it, I focused for a moment on the sensation—on the fact that there was a sensation—and I compared it to the feeling of finally being close to Dolores.

"No," he answered, momentarily surprised. "But then I suppose it's a valid question. How would you know?"

"But then who did she mean?"

He dropped shards of glass from the dustpan into the trash and came around the wide eat-in table to stand across from me.

"Do you know an Emma?" I asked, dabbing at the petroleum jelly I'd applied to my lip to stop the bleeding.

"Not that I recall, no." He waited for me to explain, his gaze on my lips. "It's something Dolores said, isn't it?"

This time it was I who waited, curious to see his intentions clarified. He took a few steps back around the table, and the distance he put between us made me trust him.

"We don't have a kitten either, and she's always calling after one."

"But she did," I answered quickly, coming around to rest against the same side of the table. "When I was with her. That one's true."

His smile was as faint as the light above our heads. When for what seemed the first time since our meeting he looked at something other than me, it lasted only a moment.

"I thought we'd have children by now," he said, and I couldn't help but grieve for him. "I didn't expect that the nanny would be for her."

The house creaked in reply, or as though under the weight of the women upstairs. After surveying the ceiling, Lyman looked to me and I realized how close we now stood to each other.

"Losing you changed her," he said, his breath near enough to brush the edge of my nose.

"How could you know?"

"You don't have to be modest, Elsie."

He'd heard me. He'd been listening when I told Dolores my name. "We're none of us to blame. It isn't your fault she's turned out this way any more than it's Dolly's fault she can't be more like you."

I waited to hear what he was innocent of, certain that there was something and that he'd only begun with Dolores and me so that it would not seem like confession.

"I'm not to blame for being uncomfortable at the sight of you both, side by side. I couldn't know what the old bird would do when I let you come inside alone. I wasn't ready to see you together, but neither was he."

I knew he meant Dolores's father.

"I would've been pleased for Dolores to see you again—I want you to know that. Cheapen her reputation, indeed. Even had that been true, it would've been his concern alone, not mine. But Dolly'd already forgotten. It was extracted, I mean, taken. And anyway, he's the only one who had a say."

When I stood erect, he followed suit and closed the gap I'd tried to establish between us. This time it was intentional.

"I'm not trying to upset you, Elsie, I'm trying to help you understand. To show you that I do."

I didn't move when his fingers traced my arm as though he'd done it a thousand times. But I knew there was a danger in him believing that he had.

"My God. Look how you've changed just since coming home. Look at the way your skin glows." He'd noticed how my color had changed since meeting Dolores, but I would not tell him why. Lyman wasn't Walter's extract, he wasn't his wife's overworked attendant, but I could feel the tension rising through my shoulders just the same.

"There's something about you that she never was; never from the moment I met her was she so sure of anything—of herself—as you are. That's how I know what you are. You aren't a memory, Elsie—Dolly's missing more than that."

"I am," I said, despite myself. "I am a memory."

"You aren't," he insisted, shaking his head, both his hands on my arms now. He wore something like a smile, but it was pained, as though he'd been working this out alone for too long and now he needed something more from me than I could comprehend. "You're whatever happened in her that morning, and your father—who didn't know better—had it taken out. You're the realest version of Dolores. You're everything she could have been from that moment on."

"It was a split second, Lyman."

"Then that's all I want. It's all I'm asking for. A moment. Isn't that what makes a man, what makes you something else entirely? One moment and how we respond?" he said, his voice hoarse and low.

"I don't disagree," I said, turning my head away so as not to speak directly into his face. When his hand rose to caress my cheek, I snatched his wrist. "I would suggest then that this is one of them."

His face fell and he shrank back, holding his wrist in the other hand as though I'd wounded him.

"I am not your wife, Mr. Shepherd. And I am not her Mem."

He backed away, his glassy eyes transparent now. This was the first time I stated aloud what I knew to be true. And Lyman Shepherd was unsurprised.

"I know," he said.

"Good. But you'll get no prize for knowing."

He stepped back even farther from me, like he might leave without ever turning around. Instead, he stopped.

"I can make sure you stay this way. That you are Elsie forever." His brow buckled as though I'd kept him waiting an impossible time. "I can make sure you are never changed, do you hear me?"

"I hear you, Lyman." It was his skin that changed then, turning damp and pale before me. "You can make sure of that, I'm aware. You must know that's why I'm here. But you will spare me or you won't; either way, you'll get no payment from me."

My entire body clenched tight, threatened for the second time in my short visit to the Shepherd house. But my Source's husband seemed to crumble then, and the next moment Lyman was gone, disappeared into another faintly lit room. When I was alone, I breathed free.

Leaning against a column on Lyman Shepherd's porch, I waited. For Dolores to awaken somewhere inside the house and fill the late afternoon with screams. For Lyman to come and find me once he'd collected himself—or hadn't. I didn't worry over the unlikely reemergence of Dolores's attendant, because pride I understood.

I looked out from the hilltop, as quiet as the valley below. Every breath was even, but more than that. It was easy, like the contentment of revealing a winning hand. It was never pure—at least not when I'd actually beaten Camille and the Professor at mah-jongg; my winning hand had always been made up of multiple suits. But there it was, the tiles arranged together in a kind of order that meant triumph, that meant I'd made sense of fate and happenstance.

This new confidence was the same, made up of heartache and joy and every good and painful thing. It was made up of my parents and fair-weather friends, of Ettie and the Vault and Harvey, too. All the things anyone had been sure I must be, however well-meaning, and all the ways I'd tried to oblige. It was made complete by seeing my Dolores again, seeing that a spark remained. What she gave to me eclipsed the feel of my silk robe, of needing to wear my name on my chest. It meant the truth was inside of me now; it swam beneath my skin, a calm and calming victory for an audience of one. It was for me and only so many as I decided to tell—and I was glad that my Dolores knew. That her husband knew as well meant nothing at all.

When a billow of dust rolled up the solitary drive as if escorting the automobile in its midst, I was ready to leave. With one final glance over the valley, I walked to the gravel road to await my chauffeur's arrival.

"Elsie," Harvey said before coming closer.

My calm still intact, I waited for him to speak again and explain why it was he who was collecting me and not the Professor. But something changed in his demeanor, his face blanching before I felt his fingertips lightly touch the skin beneath my bruised left eye and my busted lip.

"Oh." I sighed, trying to smile.

"Who did this to you?"

The question itself upset him, and he closed his eyes before I could reply. He shook his head once, his jaw clenching as if the two gestures were connected.

"Elsie, who did this?"

Taking his hand from my face, I held it in mine.

"It's nothing. It's over and done with now."

"It isn't nothing, Elsie." He tightened his grasp before letting go of my hands and bounding off toward the front door. "Lyman!"

"Harvey, no." I hurried in front of him as he continued to yell and pressed against his chest until he finally quieted down. His pale eyes were angry, black hair collapsing against his forehead the way Lyman Shepherd's never would. I hadn't thought what else to say, and a moment later Harvey pressed forward again, toward the house. I leaned into him, at first to keep him from leaving me, and then suddenly to kiss him. To calm the lines between his eyebrows and fasten us together. To finally trace the back of his neck, the groomed space so stark below his dark hair that it looked inviting even as he walked away.

After a moment, his hand was on my back and he must have felt me smile before we parted. The way he looked at me then put an ache in the very pit of my stomach. Each time his hand moved, slowly rubbing a small circle, something small and lovely fluttered inside me where the cold had once been. And then his jaw clenched again and he stepped away from me.

Lyman was in the doorway, in the same dark place where I'd first seen Dolores.

"It wasn't him, I promise," I said to Harvey before looking back to the porch and wondering how long Dolores's husband had been standing there. "I would tell you if it had been."

I explained quickly what had happened inside the house and that there was nothing to do, even as I realized there was a good chance Lyman had seen our kiss. I would never know. Cloaked in the shadow of his Queen Anne estate would be the last time I saw the man. And in it, I witnessed his true age at last. More than just the nineteen years between our first intended meeting, and now it was the heaviness of the balcony and gables of the home sagging above him and all they carried.

"I'm no monster," Lyman called out, and at first I could think to do nothing but shrug.

"Fine," I answered him from Harvey's arms. "But I won't be back."

He knew.

A timid breeze swept past me when I opened my mouth next, and of the things left to say, I could not decide between them. Because he *did* know: I was not the woman he'd married and he would have kept me just the same. There was something else hiding in the shadow across Lyman's face, and as the sun retreated further and he disappeared from view even though none of us moved, I spoke the last words to pass between us.

"If you love her, Lyman, or ever did, you won't let it happen again."

I should have said something more. Before descending the hill—instead of admiring Harvey's pale eyes and letting him lead me back to the car—I should have told Lyman to let the other woman go as well. She might have heard me, skulking behind some window overhead, tucked behind the curtain so as not to see me again. If I'd spoken, perhaps it would have shamed her into leaving on her own. But I made a choice, for me. I knew my name once and for all, and if I was not a memory—not an Extract No. 1 or otherwise—then their lives were no concern of mine.

"Don't take me home," I told Harvey when we were in the car.

"Where should we go?" he asked, and something constricted in my chest.

"I don't care. Just not back to the Vault. Not yet."

The Rialto Theatre was exactly as Camille and I had left it. Its wide and extravagant face still commanded such attention that the torch-shaped sign bearing its name was dwarfed by the building it was meant to advertise.

Parked along the sidewalk in front of it, Harvey and I sat in the car as it idled, neither of us having spoken since we left the Shepherd house. A woman and her escort passed on the sidewalk beside me, their laughter drawing my attention before the unexpected feeling of Harvey's hand brought me back to him.

"At least tell me what it was like," he said before I'd had time enough to enjoy his skin against mine. "If you won't tell me everything."

And though there was plenty to tell him, there almost seemed too much. Not because I suspected him of being too academic, as I had before. But a sea of memory, feeling, and thought could not be reduced to a few words, not well. There seemed no way at first to make it clear—how seeing Dolores and saving her from fracturing completely had solidified my name.

"I can't," I said, and he dropped his eyes because he'd expected my refusal. "Harvey, don't misunderstand.

There's no one I'd rather tell—but it's too great a thing to translate."

He looked at me again, this time with relief.

"For now I can tell you of her mind, which we both know you'll have some use for. I can tell you how she's damaged, but also so clever! She knows she isn't whole and she creates logic as she goes, to make up for what's been erased."

My chest swelled before I realized that I needed a deep breath, and I was too excited to look at any one thing for very long. On the other side of the windshield a blur of evening coats and stoles mingled with the sight of a surprising Dolores, standing at my defense. She was so different from the fractured Sources I had seen. If Harvey's father could see her now, his wondering over which of us was special might have renewed itself.

When I didn't hear Harvey's voice, I turned to him again. He hadn't asked yet what I meant, had not begun to murmur or muse, probing me to decode all that I'd observed. He was a Banker, but something kept him quiet. I saw a glimpse of it in the heaviness crowding his eyes.

"She's trying to make sense of the world, so she draws the cleverest conclusion she can. She made me a younger sister, for instance, to explain to herself our resemblance. In someone with a different, more organic condition, it would mean little—but in a fractured mind where we're used to seeing voids that can't be refilled? It's nothing short of amazing. *She* is, despite all the bits she's lost."

Harvey gave a gentle grunt and a smile. "Who's the scientist now?"

"Is that so surprising? I've been surrounded by your kind my entire life."

He nodded a concession, after which our quiet allowed the life outside to seep into the car, a trickle of laughter and a snippet of conversation sliding in the space between us.

"Was it what you expected?" he asked.

"No." I did not hesitate. "I expected her to be properly fractured. To fit within that definition with nothing left over. But why should she when I never have. Or I suppose it's the other way around."

"I don't imagine I can ever make it up to you. After what I said." Harvey gently squeezed my hand, and despite the warm cocoon of his palm and the recent memory of the kiss I'd given him, my heart shrank back a little.

"You weren't the first," I said.

"I'm sorry, Elsie. I am. I know it hurt you dearly because seeing it hurt me back. But I can't—I couldn't ignore what I know. That you're not—that you're a memory. That I don't know how long you'll live or whether I should entertain the thought of children."

When my eyes widened, his mimicked the gesture in such a helpless way that I couldn't help but have mercy on him.

"I can't be angry with you for having the same questions I did," I confessed. "I thought the man who loved me would know the truth about me—but it was Lyman who understood."

The name still ruffled him.

"I hadn't wanted to fool myself before I knew for sure, so I took you at your word. You are, after all, a learned man," I said, letting us both smile a moment without saying how he'd almost convinced me that my entire being was a matter of science. "But we were wrong. That isn't what I am. I am something new, and it makes sense that Lyman could tell, having lived with Dolores for so long. Of course he would know that I'm not a reflection of something passed."

"I would do anything to take back what I said, to be the one who really saw you." When he raked his fingers through his hair, he only managed to pull it out of place. "I knew you were something more, I swear I always did."

"I believe you," I said. "I do. But inside the Vault, your imagination could only go so far. And being at a loss for explanation just couldn't sit well with you."

"We're not in the Vault anymore, Elsie." I'd never heard him so insistent, his voice so full of emotion. "If you'd only tell me now..."

Whatever he was going to promise, whatever he hoped to convey could be different now, he must have lost his nerve. Or perhaps he couldn't forgive his previous failings, so could not imagine that I would either. Whatever the case, Harvey was quiet when the last bit of sunlight slid below the skyline as evening fell.

"I'm more than a memory," I said, and my skin tingled as though being embroidered with the evening. As though my name would appear on it, as on my cherished robe.

"I am Elsie, Harvey Parrish, not Dolores. And I am an epiphany."

Neon lights flickered against the windshield before steadying into a brightness so strong that it seemed to shine from everywhere. Pouring through the windows, the automobile grew warm inside this light and, beneath the beaming sign, so did I.

"I began as one epiphany and I never stopped having them; I've been having them all along, growing brighter every time while other Mems fade and expire. Real people have glimpses of me, realizations they then digest—the moments fade or time erodes them. But I *am* a realization, separated from Dolores before I could be changed." I thought of her then, of the dim lights in her kitchen and of the things that Lyman said. "No matter what her father hoped, extraction means I cannot be forgotten."

While I reintroduced myself to him, Harvey's face had flushed and, though they managed to hold the tears back, his eyes focused on me like they expected to see nothing after.

"You're afraid because you're not sure how long I'll last," I said while he pressed my hair behind my ear. "Neither am I. For all we know, I might never expire."

It was true. I hadn't thought it before as I waited on the Shepherds' porch, but now the thought terrified me. The world outside us reappeared and the glow became too bright.

His reply was perfect, the way he looked like he could easily laugh or cry and he found new ways to admire my face with his hands. But there seemed little consolation in his accepting my true identity and in taking me at my word if it didn't mean we were the same. And now I knew for sure that we would never be. Even the nearness in our age would soon change. I was nineteen, as I always would be. He was aging by the day, by the second. No matter how I imagined it, in how many ways—from whatever angle it was studied—there was no future for Harvey Parrish and me.

I didn't recall taking back my hand but found them both upon my chest, rising and falling in a deceptively steady rhythm. I was trapped in a web I'd thought could free me. Reviewing the conclusions I'd stumbled into, my mind reversed only to be cornered again. Because if anyone could think his way out of this, Harvey would have done so by now.

"I don't know why I came here," he was saying then, as though to the steering wheel. His nose crinkled when he strained to look up through the windshield at the torch of the Rialto. "I guess because I've never been. I never had anyone to bring."

My thoughts were halfway back to the Vault by then, somewhere between despising and envying the Mems who roamed its halls and had never wanted something they could not have. There was only one chance of being more like them.

"I thought perhaps before I took you home, we might take in a show."

I kept imagining that Dolores might still be escorted into the clinic and I into the lab with her. I could share this evening with Harvey, this final occasion of being Elsie, before a new memory was laid over me, shattering the resilience of an epiphany that had given me nineteen years and then—in one day—taking everything away.

"You must have been here a dozen times," he was saying. "Your social life has always been so much livelier than mine."

"I came here once, with a friend," I said while I could still remember, and then I forced my voice above a whisper. "And I learned that they don't forget it all. Part of the extracted memory stays behind, or at least the feeling that went with it. Even when they extract us, they're never really free."

If we were at the Vault, he might have written it down in his breast pocket notepad, flipping through the pages while he idled in my dorm. Maybe when he saw her and while preparing us for reprinting he would think that was all I'd seen in Dolores and I wouldn't be able to explain.

"None of us will be free of you," he said. "Even when we're gone."

The smile set a glimmer in his eyes and I was sure. We had traded sides completely. The truth had given him hope and had stolen it away from me.

"We can leave, Elsie. Together. Tonight."

"Harvey."

"You never have to go back inside the Vault—there's no reason to take the chance."

"You'd lose everything. I'm too important not to be missed, remember?" I said, trying to smile.

"You're too important not to last," he insisted. "Whatever happens to me, at least I'll know these memories will last forever in you."

"Nothing has to last forever," I said, my heart still breaking that he could not.

His hand slipped behind my neck, his fingers sliding into my hair while he pulled closer to me. He pressed my copper waves away from my cheek again and admired the color of my skin, his pale eyes studying me as though his memory was not the one he could rely on. Finally he kissed me, closing his eyes before I closed mine. His palms were dry, his breath steadfast. It was not the dramatic kiss of new love, when the eyelashes flutter and hands roam adventurously. The last kiss Harvey and I shared—the one he gave me back—was certain. It was a kiss for which there was no comparison, even on my beloved silver screen.

NO.10

When a day had passed without word from Lyman Shepherd and I could not spend another hour in my quiet dormitory, I sought out the Professor and the distraction of his work. In the Vault, the most intriguing development was often bittersweet, and the Keepsakes were no exception. The trio had indeed been a creative inheritance, but they did not last.

We learned that the dowager lived in a vault of her own now, overtaken so rapidly by dementia that she'd been placed in a convalescent home. Not only was she not deceased, but her executor had barely been made aware of her decline before one of her children was requesting that the Mem bequeathed to him be made available for reprinting.

"I assured the Bankers it was nearly hopeless," the Professor explained. "But they were intrigued by the unusual nature of the Mems and couldn't be dissuaded."

"You see, you're not the only one who laughs in the face of reason."

"I'll admit," he said. "It's a relief to have company in that. And more than a relief to have my concerns settled."

He must have meant that his suit against Dolores had been resolved, even if neither it nor the matter of what to do with Mems like Walter No. 17 had gone the Professor's way. He said he wouldn't be in court again, that the proceedings had stopped for good and there was nothing more to do. Perhaps that warranted relief, no matter the outcome. An equally disappointing judgment had quickly followed with regard to the Dowager Keepsakes. Though the Bankers had hoped to continue studying the three together, investigating whether their trio would continue to defy Mem expectancy because of their proximity to one another and in extraction, the court had not ruled in their favor. The Keepsakes were property, individual inheritances to the dowager's three children, each of whom could do with their Mem as they pleased.

"It seems no one outside the Vault is prepared to call into question what a Mem can be. There is no judge in this city prepared to set a precedent by distinguishing one Mem from another, as I'd hoped they would have done with you."

"You mean with Walter's Mem."

"No," he said. "It isn't something I could have spoken of until now. Even the night I asked you, my hope was too fragile to say aloud why I wanted you to extract a Mem of your own."

I wanted to ask what had changed between that night and now; his spirits seemed unreasonably high for all the refusals he had faced.

"But you were right, after all. Or anyway, it wouldn't have been as simple as I imagined to separate you from this place and from the others, in the eyes of the law."

"We cannot be real people while we have a Source," I told him gently, wishing I'd put the words in that order sooner and had told the same to Harvey. To my confusion, he'd been away all day, another Banker taking over his rounds, and by the time he returned, it would likely be too late. "And there is no escaping that Mems belong to their Sources and no one else."

So there was nothing to be done when almost immediately the dowager's son scheduled to reprint his Keepsake with a memory of his own. The Mem would no longer be a living tribute to the delicate start of his parents' love story, capturing when a young man first declared his intentions on the stoop of her father's house. When the procedure was done, she would no longer be a girl at all. Though her shell would remain the same, her spawning memory would be replaced, reprinted so that the dowager's son needn't worry over the unfortunate consequences of overextraction. I imagined Harvey's intrigue at the potential for research in a Mem whose reflection would not match its memory— if the phenomena didn't expedite the poor creature's expiration so severely that no research could be done. But research was not the law's priority, and the wish of the dowager's son was granted before the ink on the ruling could dry.

His was the first of the Keepsakes to expire, while Bankers and nurses hovered about the Mem, feverishly documenting its every confused lurch and shudder, the way it writhed and frothed at the mouth, its face pained by a congestion that could not be relieved. Its raven braid lightened and the color in its skin dried out. It happened so quickly that we could not afford to look away. The sight was remarkable, even to the now-twin clones, and they gathered around the third, drawn outside of themselves by the draining of life from their companion. It was as if they came to life long enough to see why they would die. Clinging together in the center of the crowd, the three reminded me of a tiny bouquet clutched in a hand. Only the first was reprinted, but inexplicably, one and then the other expired, losing color and wilting side by side, until a bright spot was gone from the Vault. Contemplating an endless life without their uncharacteristic whimsy, on top of everything else I couldn't have, I was all the more certain that my sanest option was to save Dolores once again.

In my dormitory, I sat at the edge of my bed with the notebook Nurse Ettie had given me, recording my memories, experiments, and observations, so that they would not be lost with me. So that when I was no longer myself, when another memory had taken my place, someone would know I'd once had a mind of my own. My sweet friend Ettie, perhaps. The Professor and Harvey might return to these pages and remember me. And as I devoted myself to their record, my epiphanies continued, as though they would to the very end. Even while watching the Keepsakes defy every established fact about the limits and uniformity of all Mems aside from me, I had another.

"You must take into account the circumstances of their extraction," I told the Professor, bursting into his office upstairs in the clinic that evening, my notes in hand. "We never have. We've paid so much attention to the nature of the memory that we've overlooked how much the Vault shapes them."

I was speaking quickly, looking from the notepad, rattling off my considerations before my time ran out.

"The Mems born into community, the ones who join a sort of collection, surrounded from the start by their Sources' memories—aside from those reprinted, they last. And more than that, they exhibit attributes not shared by other Mems, even those born into a tribe of their own."

The Professor was smiling, and while I fought the distraction of wondering why, he approached.

"Professor, are you listening to me? I am not the only unique Mem. I've seen it myself ever since I arrived. The same excessive extraction that makes a Source fragment makes a multitude of Mems who together may thrive."

"Ma petite," he said, and took my face in his hands as he was wont to do. The joy in his eyes couldn't have resulted from fatherly pride in me, in my thesis and conviction, though I detected some of that as well. "You will make a fine scientist. But I think your time is better spent preparing to choose a new home."

"What do you mean?"

"I mean that this nightmare of ours is over. You are the only Dolores left."

"I've long been," I said, timidly, so that I did not misunderstand.

"I mean that you're free."

Around the edges, my eyesight dimmed, the darkness creeping further in until the light was as faint as it had been in her parlor. It did more than mute my vision; the knowledge packed my ears, muffling everything the Professor told me next while it replayed what he'd said before. That it was over for good. How else could he have known that, had not the old attendant smothered Dolores the night before, only hours after my leaving?

She'd carried the pillow taut in the grip of her slender hands, her joints swollen with age and arthritis. The woman had come calmly down the hall and killed Dolores while Lyman slept in the same bed. She rang the authorities herself, then retreated to her room to pack her few belongings. And when the officers arrived, Lyman Shepherd awoke a widower. In a matter of weeks he would return to the Queen Anne estate of his birth and the attendant—who had finally made her own escape from the home—would finish her days in the asylum at Saint-Jean-de-Dieu.

"I didn't want to tell you until he'd put it down in writing that you are free. Dolores, he's legally relinquished ownership!"

The Professor beamed, but only I had seen Lyman Shepherd in his kitchen. Only I had heard how easily he might have decided something else. Taken me with him, or destroyed me for knowing him as well as he knew me.

"I am sorry for the loss of the young woman, I truly am. But it's difficult to imagine a better resolution for us," he said. But I could. An improbable one perhaps, but had I written it, my happy ending would have involved Dolores surviving in spite of them all—her father, her husband, and her attendant.

"Are you happy?" I asked, gently taking the Professor's hands away. I was not ready to celebrate, my tragically bought freedom or the way it changed nothing for Harvey and I.

"I'm relieved, ma petite," he said, the distinctive sobriety returning to his voice. "I'm only ever relieved."

In 1926, Le Château Apartments came to life in the Golden Square Mile, a spectacular addition to the city's skyline. A jewel of French architecture, it rose more than a dozen stories, a collection of half turrets and gable peaks adorning the building's facade and crowned in green copper. It was a castle, and the first time we stood before it, our heads fully tilted to take in its staggering height, Ettie and I decided it was home before our tour even began.

"I'm staying here," I'd promised Camille, squeezing her short and wide frame. "For good. I wouldn't go anywhere."

"Not even to see the world?" she asked between sniffles. "You can do anything you want now," she said, thinking the portion of Dolores's estate that Lyman left for me was the freedom I had gained.

"What I want is peace of mind. For all three of us." I nodded. "And we have that now." I didn't tell her about the wilted bouquet of the three Keepsakes or the epiphany they'd spawned; all that mattered was that the same not be our fate.

"And what about her family?" Ettie asked while we inspected the flat's guest bathroom, as if I would find any criticism for a private one after the lonely communal life I had led inside the Vault. I closed the medicine cabinet and watched my friend through the mirror. "Are you still concerned with their fate?"

"I can't help it," I said, turning my eyes on my own reflection. "They have lost a child."

I'd seen them in the cemetery after Dolores was gone and buried. I'd stayed away from her funeral, afraid that my presence might offend, but on December 7, 1925—on what would have been Dolores's thirty-ninth birthday—I had to be there. Ettie had offered to accompany me, but I'd insisted on going alone. Perhaps I knew that they would be there, or one of them at least.

"It won't snow," her mother said when she saw me. "It hasn't for days and I so hoped it would for her."

"She always wished for snow on her birthday," I said, careful to keep my distance, though I was surprised at how both her parents made room for me in front of the headstone.

Her mother looked at me then, eyes shimmering with anguish.

"She did." When the tears fell down her face, she looked pleased with me. "You won't forget?"

"No," I said, taking the hand she offered. "I won't forget."

And while we stood together, the lightest flurry began.

Now, months later, Ettie and I rejoined my adopted parents in the empty living room. Inside this newly finished apartment, nothing remained from before my time in the Vault, none of the possessions from the flat that the Professor had sold.

"We'll buy it all again." Camille was surveying the spacious floor plan, turning in circles as she fluttered through the house. She stopped every so often to admire a molding or frame and then beamed her infectious smile at me.

"No," I said. "I'll buy it this time." Standing at the living room window, I imagined the drapes Ettie and I would choose to decorate it and my heartbeat surged to a gallop. Whatever it had cost, I could not be repossessed now. I had no Source, so I finally belonged to me.

And then the Professor was close beside me, his neck rolled forward to bring his head low. I knew a whisper would follow—but instead, his mouth opened and then closed again. Only when he nodded once did I see the sealed envelope in his hands.

I accepted it curiously, but the Professor would say nothing; he only nodded again before leaving me to find and distract Camille, Ettie following behind.

Elsie.

I heard Harvey's voice read my name from the envelope. I couldn't have recognized his handwriting when this letter had been written with so much more care and patience than any of his scribbled notes, but it didn't matter. I knew it was from him.

I love you.

That isn't the memory that I'll extract today, I give you my word. That, I've known for some time.

My breath was stopped by a wave of dizziness. I reread the lines, first the top, the one with which he'd chosen to begin, and then the foreboding one. When I caught myself against the window, I thought I might fall through it and tumble to the busy street below.

Thank you for sharing so many of your memories with me that night outside the theater. I saw a part of you my father could not have captured in a million notes or photos. It was something all our study would never have suspected—and it prepared me for what will come next. The way I'll still remember how that night felt, even if I can't remember why. Even if I don't remember who you honestly are.

Again, I stopped, forced myself to look through the window to keep from continuing too quickly. Instead I felt the dryness in my throat, remembered his hand on the back of my neck.

I won't write it down, only this and this you mustn't share, not even with the Professor or Camille. I needed time, to keep the memory with me for a while, but now I'll keep safe what makes you so exceptional so that no one can force you underground again, even to study. Everything else, I know you will keep.

The hand against the window was cold now. When it wiped the curtain of tears from my cheeks, the fingertips were bright red, the nail beds a lavender hue. In my other hand, the letter fanned the air so that I knew I was shaking.

I will buy a desk today, I would say to Ettie when she returned, pressing my eyelids shut so that a hot seal of tears was trapped there only to spill as soon as I opened them. *I will buy a desk, and in the desk will be a drawer, with a key, and I will keep this letter there forever.*

If I were a real girl, I might have been certain Harvey loved me because he'd said so. But I was not a real girl; the brown of my skin brightened in that moment but didn't pale, and it was proof. This new epiphany would extend my life indefinitely like the ones that came before it.

He loved me. I knew for sure not because of the number of ways he'd tried to solve my predicament. I knew because he'd tried at all. Harvey Parrish was a scientist. What more provocative study could there be than how reprinting would change the famously conscious Mem—and he'd never shown the slightest curiosity.

Away from the window, I chose the alcove into which that desk would fit. I imagined how often I would sit there when the snow that had not come today finally swirled outside my window and there was not enough mink to keep me warm, when the next epiphany came and promised that I would someday be all alone.

"I will buy a desk today," I told them, when Ettie, Camille, and the Professor came back from touring the rest of the flat. Camille's round cheeks were rosy with enthusiasm and excitement; she couldn't see the way the Professor's forehead wrinkled while he towered beside her, but I could. He wouldn't know everything—not even Ettie would—but he would know what I'd lost. And he would not begrudge me a secret or two.

All the way back to the clinic, I held the letter inside my beaded purse, one glove removed so that I could at least feel the envelope he'd held that morning.

"May I wait in the car?" I asked the Professor when he'd helped Camille from her seat and Ettie had returned to the Vault.

"We'll only be in my office a moment," he answered, offering me his hand. "And then you'll never have to visit again."

I consoled myself that I'd never seen Harvey Parrish in the Professor's office. Nothing in the room would destroy me, the way the courtyard might, the way the halls and the Vault and the sitting room might unravel the fabric of me. And after today, I would keep my distance, for both our sakes.

It was a plan I felt confident would suffice until he walked through the office door.

"Hello, Elsie," he said, his pale eyes shimmering.

"Hello. Harvey." I stepped toward him and then stopped. He looked exactly as he had the night we'd kissed, when I couldn't match his happiness. "Harvey?"

The Professor put his hand on my shoulder. "Extract No. 1."

My lips parted as though I might speak to the man approaching me, but I didn't. When he arrived, I only drew in my breath further, and he didn't hesitate to gently slide his hand behind my neck, his fingers in my hair.

I stepped back.

"Harvey," I whispered to the man who wasn't there.

His fingertips found me, and then his eyes. Not Harvey's; not the man I'd kissed outside Dolores's blue-gray Queen Anne. The man who'd commissioned stained glass in a Vault dormitory before I arrived, whose touch softened when I told him I could feel.

The man whose father warned him against ever becoming a Source. And now he had.

"Elsie," the man in front of me said, and my trembling stopped. Despite that he was not that Harvey. Despite that, because he knew me, *that* Harvey might somewhere be more like Dolores than any of the insufferable, gossiping Sources.

He *might* be. I couldn't know.

I glanced back at the Professor, whose brow lifted like an invitation, and then I looked away. He knew too much—the things I'd refused to do and all the things I'd endured. There was too much to explain—worry and melancholy and the unstoppable joy blooming in the midst of it all.

"You're a Mem," I told Harvey, stepping close enough that he could hold me again.

When he spoke, he whispered the words into my ear because he knew it was a secret, and I could hear his smile.

"I'm more than a memory," he said. "I'm an epiphany."

I let my head rest against his, and when I closed my eyes, the whole world went bright.

"So am I."

AUTHOR'S NOTE

One of the most rewarding aspects of writing speculative fiction is infusing magic and whimsy (and, of course, devastation) into a world not always unlike my own. In *Mem*, I was guided as much by my love of speculative science and the myriad potential outcomes as I was by my love of Montreal. As one of many to adore the architecture of this beautiful city, it made sense to set Elsie's story during the vibrant decade during which so many gems were built (or, in the case of Windsor Station, repaired), and I so enjoyed injecting some of the unique city's history into the narrative.

One aspect of Montreal, and indeed Canadian history, that I intentionally omitted is the reality of racism that was and is present. I refused to be beholden to this ugliness, stifling Elsie's existence even further by dealing with the accuracy of how her blackness would have been treated, whether her family's wealth would have allowed her entry into the social elite, and in fact whether the Professor would have been allowed to practice in a hospital or clinic at all. While some are of the opinion that fantastical works should be free from such considerations, and while I would generally agree, I am painfully aware of the constant and seemingly universally accepted misinformation about Canadian history.

It is ahistorical to claim any lack of slavery, segregation, oppression, or marginalization occurred or persists in Canada. It has been the work of many Black Canadian academics and activists to present factual rebuttals and accurate representations, but countering this culture of omission and erasure often feels impossible. I am including this note because I cannot in good conscience contribute in any way to this lie. Racism is absent from *Mem* not because it did not exist, but because I decided it wouldn't for Elsie.

If you are interested in the often omitted history of slavery and racism in Canada, I highly recommend *The Hanging of Angélique: The Untold Story of Canadian Slavery and the Burning of Old Montreal*, by Afua Cooper, as well as *Ebony Roots, Northern Soil: Perspectives on Blackness in Canada*, edited by Charmaine A. Nelson.

ACKNOWLEDGMENTS

Writing has never been a solitary experience or pursuit for me, so thank you first to Joshua, for being my first reader for the past sixteen years and for knowing all that time that this is something I have to do. Thank you to our son, Ezra, for learning by example.

Of course, thank you to Beth (or Beft, or Elizabelle, or one other she won't let me record but believe me, it's hilarious), for falling in love so hard that I couldn't help loving Elsie more. Getting your continuous and ridiculously excited messages while you read *Mem* over Christmas break that year was one of the best experiences, as a writer.

To my CP, Stephanie Sauvinet, for your generous insight and feedback and for helping me so much in the drafting process. To Constance, who inspired the revision that made *Mem* what I always wanted it to be and whose passion for the historical invigorated me. To my lovely readers and dear friends Elena and Anna and Sasha, who always understand my voice and vision.

I've heard so many stories of artists whose families don't understand what they do, and so I am eternally grateful for the fact that my work has always been supported, especially by my father, Wavery; my sisters, Anastasia and Jennifer; my best-friend-sister, Serrana; and the mama of my heart, Anne Marie.

My journey with Unnamed Press has been wonderful from the very beginning. Thank you for reading and falling in love with my story, Jennifer, Olivia, and Chris, and for believing that so many other people would, including publicity guru Kima Jones and her amazing assistant publicist, Allison Conner, at the remarkable Jack Jones Literary Arts. You've made my debut something truly special.

@unnamedpress

facebook.com/theunnamedpress

unnamedpress.tumblr.com

www.unnamedpress.com

@unnamedpress